THE

DEADWOOD

BEETLE

THE

DEADWOOD

BEETLE

MYLÈNE DRESSLER

BLUEHEN BOOKS

A MEMBER OF

PENGUIN PUTNAM INC.

NEW YORK

This is a work of fiction. Names, characters, places, and incidents
either are the product of the author's imagination or are used fictitiously,
and any resemblance to actual persons living or dead, business
establishments, events, or locales is entirely coincidental.

BLUEHEN BOOKS
a member of
Penguin Putnam Inc.
375 Hudson Street
New York, NY 10014

Library of Congress Cataloging-in-Publication Data
Dressler, Mylène, date.
The Deadwood beetle / Mylène Dressler.
p. cm.
ISBN 0-399-14805-1
1. College teachers—Retirement—Fiction. 2. Netherlands—
History—German occupation, 1940–1945—Fiction. 3. Reminiscing
in old age—Fiction. 4. Dutch Americans—Fiction. 5. New
York (N.Y.)—Fiction. 6. Retirees—Fiction. I. Title.
PS3554.R432 D42   2001   2001025280
813'.54—dc21

Printed in the United States of America

1 3 5 7 9 10 8 6 4 2

This book is printed on acid-free paper. ∞

Book design by Marysarah Quinn

FOR CARL

In ancient Egypt . . . Heart scarabs were placed on or near the chest of the mummy . . . admonishing the heart not to bear witness against its own master on judgment day.

ARTHUR V. EVANS AND
CHARLES L. BELLAMY,
An Inordinate Fondness for Beetles

THE
DEADWOOD
BEETLE

C H A P T E R

1

WHEN I FIRST FOUND my mother's battered little sewing table—or rather, first asked the silver-haired woman who managed the antiques store, or rather that section of the tenth floor with its expensive, museum-quality French provincials, near the back of a building on West Twenty-fifth Street, in a room lit by pools of halogen light, what exactly the homely little table *was*, and what on earth it was doing there, tucked in among all the grand buffets and elegant *secrétaires*—I was careful to keep my damp hands very still, and to look down puzzled and unrecognizing at it, blinking from under my homburg, to make clear I was stunned only that she would have anything so ordinary, so obviously anachronistic and anonymous and crude and utterly out of keeping with the rest of her very fine and select trade.

I had just come up out of the street from one of my walks. I'd only wanted to get out of the sun for a moment, to shift the weight in my canvas grocery bag, and so I had browsed up the floors of the building without thinking. I went into the shop—Lowenstein's Fine

Antiques and Reproductions—for no better reason than that for the moment it had seemed empty of customers. And then, at the end of an aisle cluttered with glassy armoires and spindle-legged vanities, dancing under my septuagenarian's eyes and those fixed, spotted lights, I saw—when I looked again I couldn't mistake it—this ghost, this small, lost thing, floating like a piece of impossible wreckage toward me.

The tall and very elegant woman manager stepped forward and answered—taking my shopping bag from my hands and setting it, firmly, far away from her crystal and Limoges—that her shop specialized in "unfamiliar" pieces.

"But this particular piece doesn't seem very remarkable." My breath caught. I hoped my words would explain my unaccountable seizing in front of it.

"No?"

"I mean—it's not French . . . is it? It's certainly not provincial. It looks rustic, of course, I can see that. But—you'll have to excuse my ignorance—it's only a kind of box, with four legs. Isn't it? Is it some kind of—primitive?"

"English."

"The wood is pine." I didn't touch it.

"Blackened pine."

"Yes. I thought so." I knew so. I recognized every gouge in its surface, every pit, the places where my mother had dug in her thimble when she needed to control her disappointment in life.

"Just an ordinary twentieth-century worktable," the manager added.

"And you acquired it . . . ?"

"From my husband. This was, for a time, his shop."

"Divorce." I wiped my forehead and nodded blankly. My thoughts were in disarray. But I told myself, distractedly, It's all right, it's all right, we marital failures form a virtual club.

"No."

"I'm sorry."

"It's quite all right. Is there something else I can show you?"

"Well, this chair, for instance." I forced myself to turn away from the illuminated end of the aisle. "*This* is striking. I can see that this, *this* is something quite unique."

"Normandy. Mahogany. Eighteenth century. Very rare."

"So why then the primitive, also?"

"Because it's unusual." She looked at me steadily. "It's a family piece."

"Is it?"

"It belonged to my husband's aunt. She was a Jew in hiding during the Second World War. Would you like to know more?"

I nodded weakly. I couldn't protest.

"She was given this table when she came out of hiding. She had nothing left. Absolutely nothing. Her parents, her family, her home—all gone. But she was given this table, at liberation, by a stranger in the street who stopped and wept and set it down at her feet. Afterwards she brought it here to New York with her. When she emigrated."

The air on the tenth floor seemed suddenly thin. My nose was running, but when I felt in my pocket for a handkerchief, for anything that could cover me, I came up empty. "And, and now," I sputtered, "you're selling it?"

"Absolutely not." She tilted her head. She was so elegant. Smooth-skinned. Perhaps in her middle fifties. She had a way of pressing her lips together that also hemmed the corners of her eyes, as if to keep the light out. "We put it here to remind people. As a kind of private memorial. More intimate than the museums. I can show you," she offered.

And now she did what she should not, in a just world, have been able to do. She leaned the surface of my mother's clumsy little sewing table over by slipping her elegant, manicured and ringed fingers into the holes, so like weevil bores, that still stippled the top if it; and kneeling down inside her skirt and against a pair of elegant black leather heels, balanced herself perfectly, steadily, against strong white calves, gesturing to me to come down with her, and look, and see what was written underneath. And pointing up to the faded imprint, read aloud:

"*Als de Joden weg zijn is het onze beurt.*"

I swallowed and stood and said as quickly as I could, "What does that signify?"

She set the table to rights, pausing to wipe its surface, as though we had sullied it, before answering me. "The translation goes, 'When the Jews are gone, we will be the next ones.' It's Dutch. In a child's handwriting. That's all we know. It's been traced, childishly, twice."

"My God." I blushed. "How . . . horrible."

"You think so? I don't. I find it's almost beautiful. Like Niemöller. 'They came for the Jews, but I wasn't a Jew, so I didn't speak up. Then they came for the Catholics, but I was a Protestant, so I didn't speak up. Then they came for me—and by that time no one was left to speak up.' Clear and honest. A child's warning."

But I felt the creases in my neck burning as if a collar of hot coals had been laid across me. I closed my eyes and glimpsed the table as I had seen it last, wheeling over my head, being carried away by a mob. Then I grew tight, defensive. As if I could have known my mother's sewing table would return, all these years later, to promulgate lies. That it would come and sit here, inviting misinterpretation, misunderstanding, in this way, lying in wait in a corner, like a frog mimicking a stone. I ducked my head away from it. But heat still radiated down my chest.

The manager was now watching me closely, so sharply that I had to think of something to say, to appear sensible. So I cleared my throat and asked, politely, why, well, why she would keep such a table—since it was, in fact, such an unusual table?—simply standing out, unremarked, with all the rest of her merchandise.

"And why not?" She opened her eyes wide. Challenging me. "I'd say it belongs *in situ*, anywhere—or nowhere—or everywhere. Wouldn't you agree?" She went on to insist—though it looked to me that something, maybe the light, pained her slightly—that, to her, there seemed to be no better place for it than here, in public, in this showroom, sitting out with so many expensive, optional luxuries; and so she had set it down, right there, on that spot, where it filled out the end of the aisle, and caught the eye, and also made the other pieces look by comparison more distinctive.

"And then it's nice also," she acknowledged me, gracious again, "to have something important to talk about, with observant customers."

"But are people," I said anxiously, suddenly desperate to get away, yet trying to appear normal and calm, turning around to the Louis XVI buffet to pick up my shopping bag filled with herring tins and bananas and Pepto-Bismol, "are some of the people who take the time to ask, and get down, and look under this little table, which you say—absolutely—isn't for sale, are, are some of these people, then, sometimes"—I challenged back—"more inclined to buy your other furniture?"

Instead of replying she turned to a silver card-holder on the buffet. And drew out and handed me her trump: Cora Lasher Lowenstein, Importer of Fine Objects.

"Antiques," she said as she walked me back toward the front of the shop, "make some people feel more grounded, Mr.—?"

"Professor. Tristan Martens."

"Professor."

"Emeritus."

"Dr. Martens, is there something else I can show you today?"

"Oh, well. I . . ."

I pretended to examine another chair, this one with a stiff, harp-like back. I traced its weave blindly with my thumb. Until my watch beeped at the end of my arm, startling me.

"You'll have to excuse me."

But just before taking Mrs. Lowenstein's hand and saying our polite good-byes, I couldn't help but turn, blinking, toward the back of the store. I even agreed with this Mrs. Cora Lowenstein that yes, yes, the little table's message spoke volumes, that indeed, of course, it was worth sharing, worth making public, at least like this, in some small, intimate way. But I knew, as we shook hands, and after I'd turned my back, hurriedly, and escaped her showroom, I knew, as only I could know, and this Mrs. Lowenstein could not, that we had not even been able to name the very different volumes of which we had, separately, been speaking. Or ventured to suggest what very different compulsions it might be that drove some people to touch their hearts and then open their wallets, to buy something beautiful, to hurry and take something precious away from close contact with that dark table.

It was then I knew that this couldn't be allowed to continue. A crime was being perpetrated on West Twenty-fifth Street. A counterfeit.

Yet the table wasn't for sale.

How, then, to steal it from her?

And then I remembered, suddenly, what it was like to be small, just a very small boy, crouching and curling with something forbidden in my bed. Longing for something that I had been told I couldn't have; longing to erase the longing by possessing the wished-for thing; and then, when this couldn't be done, when it was impossible, longing for a longing to replace the first longing, by wishing for something more powerful, for a wish that could drown the drowned wish.

This is perhaps how it is with many of us. The children of Nazis. The children of Jews. We seek to supplant what can't be. We structure our lives around a hole; we pretend, not that it isn't there, for that would be ridiculous, but that with enough effort and determination it can be overcome. And so we survive.

But all I could think to myself, as I started down the street again, hurrying, lightheaded, disbelieving, my sinuses sore and my heart racing, was this very strange thought, which unnerved me, and hurt my chest, and which was perhaps what turned me down the next street, and the next, and the next, and the next, for the following year, until this very moment, walking beside me always like a ghost prodding me with a stick behind my knees: that history left to itself, untended, orphaned, strayed, finally returns and sets up shop as best it can; for every event doesn't necessarily end with the one who makes it, but can float upon the sea, or wing through the air, fluttering, untethered, hovering above the nets at our very backs—until it is caught up again afresh, and brought to light, anew. But with untold and twisted and often unpredictable results, which in this case might be expressed thus, for the moment uselessly, troublingly, senselessly:

My family's skeleton is still doing business.

I REMEMBER THE UPTURNED ROOTS of all the purple and red and bleeding white turnips I passed that day. I remember seeing those turnips, so clearly, like nicked dolls' heads, in the wooden crates outside the grocers on the way back to my apartment on West Fourteenth Street, that early fall afternoon after meeting the tall and very elegant and sometimes insistent Cora Lasher Lowenstein.

I came in and dropped my bag on the dining table, needing to take a moment to let my heart deflate again.

My living room is small. Cluttered, though I understand everything and its place. My catalogs are stacked like termite mounds around my computer and next to my dissecting microscope. The drawers contain my collection of *Cassidinae* (a subfamily of tortoise beetles), and are shoved up under the upright display cases holding the *Buprestidae* (jewel beetles) and *Scarabaeidae*. I passed these and went into the bedroom to take off my hat and coat and to change my shirt, to sit down on the bed and work my way out of my flattened, excruciating walking shoes. Then up again to brush my teeth, to cleanse myself, as though everything were normal. I slid along in my socks on the cold hard floor. I had the sensation of wood rocking underneath me.

In every corner, in the hall, in the bathroom, in my galley kitchen, it seemed to me that I rolled and collided with the sharp corners and blunt edges of things. The gout pain moved down my right leg. I felt bruised.

I saw again the date on the *Times*, lying where I had left it that morning, folded on the counter in a shape like a jib. It was as if time, which had always seemed so straightforward, so sequential, so relentless to me, was in fact a wind that could blow you whimsically, erratically, even in circles, forcing you to tack back and forth merely to regain the present.

What an old man has to do now, I thought, bracing myself against my desk, is to stop, and sit, and think about what to do. I rolled my office chair out and rested my elbows on the pages of the *Coleopterist's Bulletin*. Would a great deal of money arrange it? A bribe? An emotional appeal? Was this Cora Lasher Lowenstein susceptible to flattery? Or an offering? But how could I get the table from her without betraying my connection to it? Because I could never admit to her, now, that I had recognized my own writing even while she was introducing me to it. I would have to create a diversion of some kind. Perhaps a fire. Or a bomb threat. Of course. And then spirit the table away, while no one was looking.

Something *had* to be done. Because a sleight of hand was being performed. A lie. A meandering, hapless lie, maybe. Unspoken crimes had been committed, nonetheless.

I hunched over my desk this way for ten minutes, my hair at my temples thin and gritty in my fingers, pondering, plucking at the enormity, the impossibility, the statistical miracle of discovering my mother's table a continent away from where she had once mended my knickers and sewn a patch on my sister's sleeve.

And then I heard my last student, Elida Hernandez, beating for her appointment at my door.

DOCTORAL CANDIDATES are like flies stuck to paper. The more determined the more they become confounded.

Elida, if I didn't act quickly, would beat and harangue and bang on until I was forced to do exactly as I was doing. I stood and buttoned my flannel shirt over the long scar on my breastbone. I walked over and undid the locks one by one, left the chain latched and opened the door just a few inches to see her flashing a new diskette in front of her wide, pre-Columbian nose. As though she believed I had been waiting anxiously for her, all day. As though I had been doing nothing, all day, but sitting and waiting for her, instead of fleeing my apartment as early as I could and combing the city in search of distraction and relief from my son's most recent, accusatory letter, only to stumble, like a wanderer cursed, into an accusation buried in a building above a flea market.

"Hello, Martens." She beamed.

"You're early." I scowled through the gap between us. "I'm not dressed."

"Sorry. I'll wait."

I turned away from her to finish closing my shirt, then came back and unlatched the chain. She shot past me like a dark arrow. Elida is fond of wearing black, and was dressed from head to toe in it that day, from her cap to her heavy stockings running down into her military boots.

"Napping a bit too much these days?" she asked, looking curiously around.

"Nothing wrong with a good siesta."

"Now don't go senile on me."

She went over and sat down in the chair I'd just vacated and booted up my computer.

"Just look at this and make sure everything's all right."

"Why didn't you just message it?"

"Because I wanted to go over this with you in person. I don't trust Blathert, anymore."

"Blathert is a good young man."

"Blathert is too wrapped up in his own funding."

Blathert's ambitions notwithstanding, since my retirement from the university the summer before, Elida had refused to take her work to her committee without my screening it first. Or to stop coming by the apartment, bringing with her new software and CDs and set-up manuals. Or to let a month pass without checking my cables and drives. Doctoral candidates are optimistic; they believe even the oldest components capable of upgrade.

Apparently it still hadn't penetrated her large, dark, heart-shaped head that I was already, because of her untiring help, set up properly to do research at home. Or that she was no longer my graduate assistant, after all. Or that now she had to discover her own life, and finish her own fieldwork, and take her obligatory turn, as I once had, standing at the head of a classroom, trying to make sense of those strange creatures, the peculiar, unfamiliar beings twitching and turning and grimacing and biting the ends of their pencils, their jaws, to my mind, always so much more frightening than the hairy mandibles of the praying mantises curled up in the Plexiglas lab dishes in front of them.

"You'll be surprised," she said.

"You don't say." Did she, I wondered, even notice my distraction?

"God." She shivered. "I love this stuff."

I came over, pulled in reluctantly by her rapture, and watched her scroll through her data, reviewing her collection sites. Sedona. Sonora. "Mexican Hat"? Why was she so attracted to tundra, to desert spaces, so wide open and arid and desolate? In comparison to other habitats, the desert, after all, can be diffident in its manner of yielding up beetles. In the days of my own fieldwork, in the jungles of the Yucatán, for example, or in the deep forests of the Amazon, we were able to shake and fog so many out of the trees it was like a rain of opals, green and gold and shimmering, fiery iridescent red, shocking blues, tumbling onto the beating sheets. A man could stand, obscured, hidden under the dense canopy with the smell of damp wood-pulp in his nose, and the coils of ferns brushing his face, and the butterflies would come when he held out his arms and land and lick the oils from his skin.

Elida, however, said that kind of research was "gluttonous."

"I've settled on Batesian mimicry," she said now, glancing over her shoulder. "I'm working on another species that avoids predation by mimicking wasps."

I peered mechanically down at the screen. Elida's entire thesis, it appeared, would be devoted to the insect deceivers. "Palatability isn't the issue," I objected. "Also, the coloration is right, but the resemblance isn't marked enough. This specimen doesn't have fly-ing wings." (This is common enough, of course, among desert Coleoptera. Most beetles have membranous flying wings beneath their outer sclerotized casings, or *elytra*. In the desert, however, con-ditions are so extreme that some species need the dead air space between their bodies and their chitinous shell, as a form of insula-tion. They have forsaken flight, evolutionarily speaking, for this cushion or shield. To sit inside their own climate control. A kind of emptiness-as-buffer.)

"It's not the design," she responded. "It's not the flight pattern."

"Well—what, then?"

"Guess."

"Don't get childish on me."

"You taught me. 'Speculate or stagnate.' Go on, Martens. *Guess.*"

I made the effort. I swear it. I did. I tried to reach down for the old curiosity, the interest, the old indulgence—the very last of my reserves—at seeing twenty-six-year-old Elida Hernandez grope toward some substantial contribution, or at least some foothold, some tiny insight into a world that contains (if Erwin's estimate of the total number of tropical Coleoptera is correct, and I am among those who believe it is) more than eight million separate species of beetle, nearly all of these still unidentified and undiscovered, unknown, unnamed, unrecognized, and unloved. Mountains and valleys and plains and rivers and lakes and farms and forests and jungles and canyons and kitchens and baseball fields all crawling with this great, impervious, aloof horde of armored, brittle-bodied life, scuttling on, uninterested in us, a minority species—while they breed and hatch and crawl and swim and fly, biodiversification's giddy excess, having definitively *gotten something right.* One-quarter of all the animals on earth. One-fifth of all living things. The most successful creatures on our planet.

Once, the numbers had soothed me.

"Sorry," I sighed. "I just don't see it."

"Well, professor?"

"Go on then. Dazzle. Enlighten me."

"It's the dance." Her eyes widened, proudly, looking at the screen. She was plainly mesmerized by her own work. "Look at Figure Two. The individual mimics the pattern of the wasp at the nesting stage. It circles and turns on fallen wood or recessed rock, confusing the observer visually."

"That doesn't seem enough, somehow."

"Wait. It gets better. It buzzes."

"Without wings? How?"

"I'm not sure. I'm speculating it stridulates using the air-space above the abdomen. Perhaps as a kind of whistle."

"You'll have to be more precise than that."

"I plan to be."

"Even so," I hurried her along, "what's the good of all this if it brings an amorous wasp down looking for company?"

"That's the best part. The wasp is the only one who isn't fooled. She scopes it out and moves off."

"Clever gal."

"Why, thank you. Check it out and see."

She moved from my chair and dropped into the sofa beside my desk, the loose cushions rising under her hips, one dark crushed velvet wing on either side. So I was forced to really try to concentrate, now. I sat and made a cursory analysis. Yes, yes, yes, it was all very good, very sound. Astute. Independent. Perhaps one or two mi-nor . . . But no, Blathert would catch the details, as her director. For the rest the chapter was quite professional and authoritative. Achieved. Balanced. Enough for me to wish, with one last, convuls-ing impulse, that I could be young again: a fresh biologist with page after page of closely observed text and footnote, her enthusiasm, her data, her deductions, her recommendations, her concerns regarding environmental degradation, genetic alterations, minor variations, et cetera, et cetera, et cetera . . . Brava. Brava, Elida Hernandez.

I had already told her, many times, that given her level of work and her grants and her connections she was assured a fine place in the profession. She simply had to get on with her conclusions. But she was never satisfied. She frowned and twitched now, nervously.

"Relax," I said. "You're in fine fettle."

"Does it seem too extravagant? Too graduate-student-ish?" She pulled her cap off, collapsing it in one hand, feeling the top of her head uncertainly with the other.

"Stop thrashing. It's like watching a frog with three legs."

"*Not* funny." She turned away, offended but distracted, tossing her hat at my hall tree in the corner.

"Missed." She swore.

"Go pick it up."

She was wearing her hair long again, in a braid, swinging like a thick split chrysalis down her back. She took things soberly, did this last student of mine. Intensely, personally. Folded them close to her skin, with a gesture that reminded me of a police officer protecting an orphan. Then at the drop of a hat she would wax ferocious on global warming, unexplained deformations in certain indicator species, and herbicidal-pesticidal agricultural runoffs.

"The temperature's too high in here," she noticed. "Let me change your thermostat."

"No. My collection. My cassidines."

"They're going to dry up and disintegrate. So are you. We need to get you out of here occasionally, Martens. Take you out to the park. For a walk. Seriously." She looked around, again considerate of me. She was solicitous when she wasn't completely consumed by her own projects.

"I don't go out much anymore." Now, I thought, if I needed an alibi during the time when Cora Lowenstein's store was ransacked, Elida could provide it. But what about fingerprints? I should wear gloves.

"So you're just sitting around reading articles all day."

"It's like heaven," I answered.

"And you're not writing?"

"A little, now and then."

"No new projects?"

"No . . ."

She caught the hesitation in my voice. Almost leaping to my side. "I knew it—you can't stop!" She said this as if she needed me to be something enduring. A monument. "What's happening?"

"I'm not really sure."

"More work on the tortoise beetles? I knew it."

"Well, yes. What else."

Disappointing. Depressing. But there it was. Even in her freshman year, she had been unswervingly, unapologetically, the scientist. Locked, as onto a target, on all things scholarly. I could still see her, in that first year, so many years ago, staking out the hallway near my office, lying in wait for me, ready to put forward the most radical theories about the white fly. She had the successful academic's hunger, even then. The ambition that narrowed life to a single stalk: a green reed to be gnawed on and chewed and grasped with all available limbs and climbed, up and up and up, until it gave out a higher view. Already she seemed to be bobbing somewhere above me.

I changed the subject. "What did you say you were going to call your specimen?"

"I haven't decided. Genus unknown. But given the behavior, I call him a trick beetle."

Of course we both knew that, for years, her little impostor would go on being listed in any photograph or index simply as *Unidentified*.

ELIDA WANTED TO DISCUSS the malformed dragonflies in Minnesota. The migration of the European butterflies as they spread northward on rising temperatures and suffusing greenhouse gases. The caterpillars of the Monarchs dying while they fed on milkweed plants dusted by pollen from stands of American bioengineered corn. Exasperated, I finally sent her downstairs and around the corner for some laser paper and ink cartridges, which I didn't need, and could just as easily have had delivered. I simply needed her to *go away* for fifteen minutes, so that I could smuggle a moment to catch up with my own unsettled ideas. And also, all right, so that she could still feel she was, in some way, "helping" me.

How to account for this tendency, in some human beings, to continue rendering service to other human beings who have, decidedly and completely, abandoned them? As social behavior, I submit it's illogical. Still—wasn't it the habit of foolish husbands who kept sending birthday cards and checks to their ex-wives in Texas, and to their religious-fanatic sons, who kept sending back ranting, accusing letters? And now, clearly, of graduate students who still showed up, unnecessarily, at the flats of their almost delirious professors.

WHEN FOR THE FIRST TIME my mother turned her back on her small village in Bavaria, and went to one of the larger towns to see actual moving pictures (American reels *verboten* during the First World War), she had stared up amazed and adoring at the aloof, distant, silent clowns, longing to be of some use to them in their troubles. Chaplin, tripping over his eggplant feet. Harold Lloyd, hanging by his pants from a gigantic clock.

"Of course, those weren't German men," she told us in her peasant's accent many years later; my sister and I were toddlers by then, playing at helping her wash stockings. "I understood even as a young girl that a German man would never allow himself to hang by his balls from a clock."

Perhaps our lives would have been different if my mother hadn't been so attracted to aloofness and clumsiness. Perhaps I would never have been born. Perhaps I would still be lying, an unfertilized clump in the honeycombs of the universe.

As soon as Elida had gone I got up and went into the bedroom and drew out my old satchel from underneath the bed. Inside, under the pictures of my wife and my son, *she* lay, dry and brittle: my mother at ten years old. Her First Communion. She stood, ankles pressed tightly together. These might have been nailed. Nursing a crucifix to her flat chest. She was all collarbone and elbows, then. A brown lamb in white. Once, crouching and hiding under her table as a boy, I had caught her bleaching her upper lip with peroxide. She must have had trouble, later, convincing the neighbors she was Aryan.

My mother, after seeing those larger, more prosperous German towns, revolted against the idea of having to grow up and settle down with her parents on a backward vineyard. The future was made clear to her, she said, in the shape of a dead calf she found when she was fourteen. To her, it was a sign from God.

"And I saw that calf," she told us, "lying there in the field. So pretty in the white flowers. With its tongue hanging out, and a rope around its neck. And I couldn't tell if this calf, she died because of the rope around her neck—or if she just happened to be wearing a rope around her neck when she died. But then, I saw—it's all the same thing. If I stayed, I was going to die with a piece of farmer's rope around my neck. So, God slaughtered the calf, children. He was speaking to me. He was telling me to go off and get my own."

I closed and slid the case quickly again under the bed. Where had Elida gotten to? She was taking so long. Really, it was a fairly simple matter to go down and buy a box of paper and not take an hour about it. When what an old man needed was to see her long, young legs in their stockings, to watch her firm, young step crossing my living room again, to see her thick young braid swinging endlessly, back and forth, like a rope that will never tangle.

Old fool, I thought. You have become sexually depraved. Or deprived. Both.

FOR A MOMENT I was alarmed at myself. Then I remembered there was nothing a man in my battered condition could do—with the tracks of scars running up and down my body like the seams that had once sent shivers crawling along the neck of Mary Shelley, and the circulation in my legs so bad the pain was like standing on two knives, and both tips pointed at my groin—nothing, nothing at all a man, of my age and beaten temper, could possibly do, should a woman—I mean, any woman other than, older than, Elida Hernandez—should any such woman ever come my way, and be tricked into spending some time with me—no, it was a waste of precious time, now, so I might as well give it up, worrying over something that would never happen.

Elida banged at the door again. I heaved up from the floor and let her in. She had stopped off at the deli for bagels and cheese, which she said she thought I might like, forgetting, as young people can, that we old ones carry around hearts like time bombs. My cardiologist had recently reminded me that cheese, in particular, is lethal. Squeezes itself like plastic explosive into a pipe.

"Elida," I said, chewing my plain bread, which tasted of nothing, while she changed out my cartridges. "You don't have to do that."

I beckoned, impatiently, unable to speak while I swallowed. She nodded and came and sat down with me at my Reagan-era glass-and-chrome dining table. One of the relics of my divorce. Its oval surface is so smoky, so scratched in the light, it's like eating from a plate of hair.

"It's not a problem," she said.

"You must have a life. Somewhere."

"You're looking at it," she said, chewing her bagel and leafing through one of my catalogs. She seemed determined. Tense. Absorbed. Herself.

"Go out and get a date then, for God's sake. Maybe we both stay in too much."

"I haven't had a boyfriend since I started collecting roaches.

You'd best keep your bugs in your drawers, too, if you're thinking of having some nice lady over for coffee, Martens." She stopped and picked up and licked the cheese from another bagel. "My experience is that most people run when you give them a look at arthropod guts. Or at the insides of any living thing. Anyway this conversation is too intimate. I'm going to tell the dean you're bringing up inappropriate subject matter."

"You're not under my direction anymore. So I'm immune."

"I'll tell my mother. No, my grandmother. She's an old *Oax-aqueña*. She'll curse you with a chicken liver."

It was usual, this sort of banter between us.

"Are you really feeling—isolated?" she asked hesitantly.

"It's my most preferred and productive state," I put her off. "Don't you have a class to teach?"

"Not until seven."

"Hadn't you better go and prepare?"

"I'm all set. Tonight it's organ systems."

"What, about fifty undergraduates? What have they been like?"

"Restless."

"You'll get used to it."

"Maybe you should get out of here, Martens. Move out. See more. Travel." She bent and looked under the table. "Feel those old legs underneath you."

"Sometimes an old man's legs have felt enough."

"So?"

"I did plenty of moving around when I was younger."

"Sure, but when was the last time you were out in the field?"

"I don't know. I don't remember—eight years, I think."

"Don't you miss it?"

"Everything has its time and place."

"Well, then why don't you go be a tourist somewhere. Go back to the Old Country. *Ja?*" She mimicked my accent. "*Sum*thing."

"*Mira,*" I mimicked hers. "People emigrate for a reason."

"Of course they do. Money."

Apart from our obsession with beetles, Elida and I had, as I was aware, only one other, incidental thing in common: we had both become naturalized citizens in the same year.

The difference, however—and I didn't forget this as she jumped up and snatched her cap from the hall tree and turned, young and healthy and strong, to go; I didn't forget, as she stooped and wiped the cheese crumbs from her thick black stockings—that *she* had had the good fortune to have been transported to this land of reinvention when she was still only a baby. She had told me, once, that her family had come to New York from Mexico when she was barely two years old. Naturally, she'd said, she could recall few attachments from before then. So. No corpses buried in a foreign soil, for her. All for Elida was right, bright, new, and fresh. Nothing miserable lay behind; nothing to be ashamed of, to hold at bay, to ward off.

"Go get some work done," I dismissed her.

As I lay in bed, later that night, unable to sleep, looking into the darkness, wide-eyed, maddened by the thought of my mother's table now, crouching out there, somewhere, in the lowered lights and long, distorting shadows of a closed and locked antiques shop, I tried to calm myself by imagining Elida still up and climbing her green reed. I watched her grasping, reaching, hand over hand. I saw her gaining a height and gazing out over the clean, red rock vistas. Her open, desert spaces. And then I was so amazed at our different destinies, at how disparate the world could be as it struck the retinae of our separate and detached existences, I was almost relieved. I turned my body, shivering, to the wall. And breathed into the space between the blanket and mattress to warm my numbed feet.

I DIDN'T GO BACK to Cora Lowenstein's store the next day. Or the next. Or the next. Not because I was feeling cowardly or unnerved, you understand. Simply, I wasn't able to decide what was the best course of action. And then, having decided, I needed some time to pull myself together.

It wouldn't do, if I was going to try to win her respect, to show up at her place of business looking out of sorts or out of control, alarmed, inarticulate, or unfocused. For several days I ate more roughage (higher bran and fewer oily herring), and performed a kind of penance by getting up early in the morning and sitting at my computer and searching out sites with information about the Nazi Party's destructiveness in Holland. For those who may not be familiar with the details of the Holocaust as they apply to the country of my birth:

Beginning in 1940, Dutch Jews were segregated from the rest of the population, particularly in schools and in higher education. They were forbidden to use public amenities, to sit in restaurants, to attend concerts, to buy ice creams, to enter shops, or to walk freely in public parks.

By 1942 all Dutch Jews living on farms or in the provinces were relocated and concentrated in the cities, where they were required to wear the Star of David. Deportation of all Jews to the death camps in Poland, by way of an "organizational center" at Westerbork, began in the spring of that year.

Prior to 1940 one hundred forty thousand Jews lived in the Netherlands. At final count, one hundred seven thousand were sent by cattle train from Westerbork. One hundred two thousand of them were killed. The mortality rate for Dutch Jewry, at seventy-three percent, was the highest in Europe.

It was in some measure due to the committed work of low-level bureaucrats that a small nation found itself, in spite of itself, the most successful at carrying out Hitler's agenda.

FOR SEVERAL DAYS I hung back, agitated, uncertain, sometimes fibrillating. My worry was that if I went back to her shop too soon, Cora Lowenstein would become suspicious, and understand my motives, and see right through me, and refuse to leave the building with me.

Then, as persistent as ever, Elida Hernandez had messaged to ask if I had any plans for later in the month, at Thanksgiving. I lied and told her I would be dining quietly with friends. And then I understood it was time to act. Because there wasn't much time left, no, no, and an old man had to do what he could to bring some order to his corner of the universe, while there was still a matter to clean up and sort out, to pack up and name and address and have properly delivered.

～

THE CONDITION OF MY HEART, while it has deteriorated slightly in recent years, still allows me to get out and walk the streets, when I have to. Often, I can even go as far as Central Park— though usually I have to take the bus back, and then sleep on the couch in front of the television for several hours, before I can stand up again. The three bypasses I received in Houston in 1983 at the hands of Dr. DeBakey were, for their time, state of the art. I have never had anything to complain of regarding Texas in *that* respect. In fact I was grateful for my makeshift arteries that nervous morning, preparing for my visit to Cora Lowenstein, looking into the hall-tree mirror and wrapping a muffler carefully (and I hoped elegantly) around my neck. Often I imagine my bypasses, as I did that day, as the obliging arms of an octopus, wrapped around me and squeezing me tightly, together, forcing my lifeblood up and over and around my defunct tissues.

It wasn't until the early nineties, and largely as the result of improper diet and some overwork and accumulated stress (the divorce and other, related matters) that my circumnavigating veins had to be "cleaned up" yet again, this time via angioplasty. With tiny balloons, probes I had thought I could actually feel filling my chest, much in the way I felt my fingers now, as I walked out the door, stuffing themselves into the channels of my stiff leather gloves.

EVERYTHING STARTED OUT well enough. I wore enough layers against my cold skin to keep the shifting autumn weather at bay. That is, I was able to keep it from every place except my face, which took the wind—though I tucked my head under my hat—from the east like a series of blows from nose to chin. I felt my cheeks turning red and my sinuses beginning to slurry. Fortunately I had my handkerchief with me, this time around, so there was no reason to think I wouldn't still be presentable, invigorated, perhaps even red and robust-looking (if in a deceptive sort of way) by the time I climbed the winding staircase to Mrs. Lowenstein's showroom on the tenth floor.

I needed to look healthy. Irresistible. Confident. Manly. Such an elegant woman, so competent and assured, wouldn't be likely to hand over a precious heirloom to a pale figure drooping, dropped from a passing taxi as though from yellow formaldehyde, his knees buckled and knocking, his legs gouty. So I walked. I carried no cumbersome bag of herring tins and Pepto-Bismol with me that morning. I walked with my hands in my pockets, stiffly, but moved my shoulders to feel them loosening, like airfoils. Soon it wasn't a matter of many blocks. I even began to feel optimistic.

It isn't true (as my ex-wife still has people believing) that since my attacks I have become reckless and fearless. That I have developed a morbid death-wish. I didn't walk that morning—I have never walked to tease my heart to the limits of its capacity, or in the hope that I would fall down in the street before my left foot had time to relieve my right. No. Never. In all those years when I jogged up the steepest hills of our Connecticut neighborhood, or took the stairs when I might have ridden an elevator, or swam in the club pool losing count of the laps—when I pushed myself, as I still do, to see how long my breath might continue to buoy me above the surface—these were all of them, all, attempts to feel alive when I wasn't quite sure I was so: when I thought my senses had beguiled me and I was, without knowing it, already in a plane of numbness and insubstantiality.

And so I walked and breathed deeply and kept my head down and knocked into the shoulders of my fellow urbanites. The city just before the holidays felt dense with compressed expectations. I circled away from a foul-smelling crate of putrifying yellow squash. I dropped a quarter in the cup of a young panhandler to keep him from accosting me.

"God bless you, man."

In a few weeks there would be tinsel above the fruit stands and lights blinking in the dry cleaners' doorways. Plastic garlands snaked around light posts, and Christmas ornaments dangling from the ears of the department-store salesgirls. Menorahs propped unlit on the casements and Santa Clauses taped, tuberous bellies in profile, in the public-school windows. And the bright colors of the African celebration, what was it called? Kwanzaa. The world entire, marking the closing of a calendar. I slowed in anticipation as I neared Chelsea.

I hadn't veered into the neighborhood on that ordinary day which seemed to me now, in retrospect, so extraordinary, because I had succumbed to a sudden need for used *accoutrements*. Rather, it had been because I hadn't yet pushed myself far enough; hadn't yet reached the point when I could feel my feet humming as they touched the cracked pavement, and my lungs expanding, colliding like twin zeppelins inside my chest. So I had hiked on and on—and it was only when I'd become, like this, a little lightheaded and confused, perhaps underoxygenated and overexposed, and heard a strange whining, like a siren in my ears, that I'd ducked in under the awning of the Chelsea Building, in the same way as I now did, quickly, because it had seemed shaded inside, and tall, and large, and narrow, and I had needed, as I do from time to time, a place from which to look quietly down at things without being seen in return by them.

"IS MRS. LOWENSTEIN AVAILABLE?"

"Pardon?"

It didn't occur to me, until that moment, that she might not be. I had been so certain of our inevitable meeting again, over the scarred and bored wood of my mother's table. It was impossible for Mrs. Lowenstein not to be "in." I required her, in fact, to have been waiting in frozen animation—suspended from invisible wires, for a week, just as I had left her, with her elegant hand poised above the table as though it were an animal and she were hovering over it, guarding it, preventing it from starting up and following after me.

The young man in the loose jacket looked at me in what I imagined was my red-cheeked, robust, virile state—his effeminate hand stilled in the act of raising a feather duster. He scanned me, up and down. And looked away. I felt exactly as though I were being tossed back on a remnants heap.

"*Ms.* Lowenstein is in the office," he said, snottily. "Whom should I say is here?"

"Dr. Tristan Martens," I said.

It's always much better, with some people, to use the title of doctor instead of professor. In the past such adjustments have secured for me better tables at dinner, greater politeness from waiters, doormen, and underlings in general, and especially from receptionists (for example, in the offices of doctors), as well as speedier invitations for my wife to summer beachhouse parties, that is, in her pre–Radical Religious Right days, when such things still mattered to her.

"I'll have Ms. Lowenstein out for you in just a minute, sir."

"That will be just fine," I said coolly. "Thank you."

I stood at the end of one aisle, where I could look down the row of scrolled armoires and potbellied vanities toward my mother's table. It sat forlorn under the spotted lights. A little child lost. I swallowed. *The wonder and pain of it being there.* The queer marvel. I edged toward it, feeling something, I couldn't help it, that must have been like the confusion and hope and longing of the woman who crept toward that improbable baby's basket nestled in among the reeds. How was it possible it could have survived? That it could be so untouched? So preserved in its wear and decay? I stripped my gloves from my fingers while I waited, head turned sideways, away from it, feigning absorption in a commode, for the appearance of Cora Lowenstein.

I had already planned what I was going to say to her. A little light banter, a veiled apology. Something about the Dutch once having owned all of Manhattan, and how it made us a bit proprietary, and profoundly interested in things. How we just couldn't help ourselves.

⌘

I FORGOT THIS, however, the moment she materialized from a corner, wending her way, tall and steady, between the armoires and clocks and tables and chairs and balanced plates, so comfortably, so easily, it was like watching a master yachtswoman shoot a narrow sound.

"I hope you will remember me?" I heard myself stammer.

She held a long hand out, nodding slowly and very elegantly. Her silver hair swept back from her forehead in a short, windblown cut. Her face was as I remembered. Pointed, like a bird's, capable of hunting, yet who no longer had to. She was almost beautiful.

"Last week." I pulled my fingers from hers and took my hat in my hands and pushed the few strands of my hair back, abashed, feeling the fragile web tearing apart at my touch. "I stepped in for a moment, and, and you showed me that table." I pointed, stoutly, in its direction.

Her eyes narrowed at me. They were green. Sea green. They appeared now to be genuinely thoughtful, engaged, no longer opaque and coolly tolerant but peeling back the days behind us, hour by hour. She was both seeing me and not seeing me. I could tell this much. I became strangely excited. She was seeing me in this moment as I stood there, in front of her, but also trying to carry me backwards, like a parcel, backwards in her recent memory, walking backwards with it herself, she was remembering now, nodding, yes, yes, a parcel, a canvas shopping bag full of groceries and books and herring tins and Pepto-Bismol, to where she had set it, right there, right there, of course, on the Louis XVI buffet far away from her Limoges plate.

"Oh, yes! From the university. Professor." She nodded and took my hand again. "I remember. You also looked at our harp chair."

"Yes. Well, technically I'm no longer at the university. I am, in fact, retired." It was important, extremely important, if I was going to get what I wanted from her, that I appear precise. Exact. Trustworthy. A man to whom you would relinquish a fragment of your history.

"Yes," I began again. "You showed me that table. . . . I haven't been able to get it out of my mind since. It's very strange. I don't know how to account for it, really. Maybe it's my age, or my nation. You know that we Dutch can't help—"

"You don't have to explain. I guessed it the other day. Did you lose many of your family in the camps?"

I couldn't close my mouth.

"I—I'm not Jewish. I was just a boy, in Rotterdam. During the war."

"Oh, I see," she said. Her eyes hemmed again. I was again a bag set aside, I saw, something large and innocuous, but steadier at a distance.

"I'd like to discuss something with you," I offered.

"Then perhaps you'd like to come into my office." I noticed once more her ringed and slender hand, gesturing as graciously and neutrally as an ambassador's.

MRS. LOWENSTEIN'S LITTLE high-ceilinged office was a clutter of small engravings, elegant lampshades, fringed pillows, an oaken desk built cunningly with bookcases into the front and sides of it, a side table with coffee mugs and a chic black coffeemaker, architectural and design magazines scattered everywhere, large unburned candles, clocks ticking and unticking, business cards in their silver holders and brown and green and blue iridescent glass paperweights in humped shapes that reminded me of the *Carabus* beetles. *Carabus superbus.* Native to France and Germany. *Carabus aurenitens.* I repeated the words in my head, to calm myself. She removed a pile of industry journals sitting in a leather chair beside her desk and invited me to sit down.

"It's wonderful in here," I said politely. "Eclectic."

"A jumble, but I don't mind."

"You must be very busy. And doing well."

She tilted her head sideways away from me; but I hadn't started yet on actual flattery. It was merely that so many of the pieces we'd passed on the way to her office weren't the same as those I had last seen in the shop. Maybe they had only been rearranged. But my mother's table hadn't moved. It was as if all the rest wheeled and spun around its fixed center.

"Business is good," she acknowledged. "Although there's a great deal of competition in this building. I manage to keep things going, at least."

"At least? You—you sometimes wish you could unburden yourself?" Here might be my opening. She wasn't old, but then she was no longer young. Perhaps fifty-five. Some obligations, I leaned forward and tried speaking to her with my eyes, some obligations are better passed on . . .

"This showroom was my husband's livelihood. To support his musicianship. He was a pianist. He played the Van Cliburn. Per-

haps you've heard of him? Sandor Lowenstein. He was a true amateur, a lover of fine things. I'm keeping it going, until . . ." She hesitated.

My chance to interrupt, to prompt.

"Until you've had enough?"

"Until something happens. Life is like that, wouldn't you agree?
Periods of waiting and storage between things that happen."

"Yes," I found myself saying more emphatically than I'd meant to.

"Yes. Would you like some coffee?"

"No. No, thank you."

"And so, what is it you wanted to discuss?" She reached for a
gilded cup and saucer. "You're thinking of a major redecoration? Or
a select investment?"

"Ah, now. Well."

I had to remain focused. I had to be confident, firm, inspiring. To
move her, by careful degrees, with my vigor and earnestness. Or—or
could I simply—admit all of it? What would happen, if I did? If I
tried to explain? Who knew, I might be out of the place with my
mother's table in less than an hour, without having to resort to a long
siege of her sensibilities, or some desperate appeal to her womanly
nature, or a low trick. It could all be settled right now. Quickly, fairly,
honestly. Between two straightforward people.

"I told you I couldn't stop thinking of the table with the boy's
writing under it."

"What makes you think of it as a boy's?"

An error already. I began to sweat.

Mrs. Lowenstein, meanwhile, crossed one long leg easily over the
other. I saw part of her white-stockinged knee peep out from under
her woolen skirt, shaded like a half-moon.

"Excuse me?" I blundered.

"I said, why do you think the writing is a boy's?"

"It isn't—it's because—I'm sensitive to—I know—handwriting has some significance."

"Are you a graphologist?"

"I meant, a personal significance."

"Yes. It's had that for quite a few people who've seen it. I remember one woman who came in and also told me it had to be the writing of a small boy. She was Korean. She said she saw the justice of the young Buddha in it. And an Indonesian once told me it was the wisdom of the boy prophet."

"And—and what do you see?"

Mrs. Lowenstein narrowed the focus of her eyes again. Holding her coffee, resting her elbows on the arms of her chair, sinking more permanently into it. "Frankly, I see all of history condensed to a pencil's point of logic and understanding. I see truth. I don't need to know whether it was a boy or a girl. I don't want to. The anonymity is what's important about it. A little wisdom doesn't need to have an author. It can be shared by everyone."

"The details don't matter."

"Truth omits details. Doesn't it, professor?"

"Some say God is in the details."

"Then they need to step back a bit."

And here I was cut dead in my tracks. Stopped by her. Stymied. I couldn't see my way around her certainty. Her assurance. Her insistence. She sipped at her coffee, swallowing with a polite, finished sound.

And all the while I was experiencing, suffering, at that self-same instant, the clearest, sharpest memories of my mother's calloused fingers snagged in my father's rough, tobacco-stained clothing, slipping and sliding her needle in and out between the dark patches. I had suddenly, too, the terrible sensation of being in too many unnamed, inadmissible places at once. For even as I saw my mother's fingers slipping and sliding inside the dense material, I imagined this Cora Lowenstein slipping her long, elegant, ringed fingers into the deep, notched holes in the surface of my mother's table, cleaning them out, matter-of-factly, adjusting accounts, as if pressing the hollow keys of an antique adding machine.

I looked down at my naked hands in my lap. What now, then? I could offer truth only at the price of hope, erase one evil only with the blot and stain of another. I felt the leather chair hard at my back, unforgiving.

"And for you," she said implacably. "The personal significance?"

I crossed my legs, to mirror hers. I had to find another way. I wasn't ready to give up. I tried to relax. Breathe in, out. In. Out. The air smelled of mocha and old brocades. I could confess, of course. Yes. Yes. But without disturbing her ideas. I could tell her, perhaps, that the sentence was partly mine, without admitting my knowledge of its context. I could be at least partially truthful. I could dance around the edges. . . . But no, no, it was hopeless. Without the conviction, the surety, the details that are the truth—the way my father shouted that day, the excitement of my sister, the set, hard face of my mother, the feel of the cold tile floor underneath my knees—how could I prove the table was mine? How would I convince?

And then I saw, further into any conversation stretching ahead of us, the lies I would be led into, false explanation on top of false explanation, error compounded by error, always, always—there seemed to be no escaping it. It was no use. I twisted against the back of the chair. And felt pinned. And angry. Yes, angry.

Who was this Cora Lasher Lowenstein, anyway, who was any human being that she shouldn't have her precious illusions taken away?

"I'm still haunted by the war," I said harshly. "I remember being in Rotterdam, and the roundups. I don't forget that."

"I know. So many people feel that pain."

"You *cause* pain," I said accusingly. "When you show people what you keep in here."

She looked at me, surprised. Erect. But still the elegant, controlled saleswoman. Still composed. She paused, and reconsidered. It seemed impossible for her ever to be ruffled, or offended, or alarmed. She wrinkled her smooth forehead patiently, considering. And suddenly I wanted to see this Cora Lowenstein tied up—I wanted—I wanted—to see her with a pink brocade coverlet knotted around her waist, dangling out of a window from the tenth story of this building while it burned. While she clung. Swinging, suspended. Exposed. The Fire Department looking up, waving frantically at her. People shouting at her to hang on, not to jump. For a moment, this image held me. Then I imagined her face—how it would still be considering, competently measuring the distance to the sidewalk, the degree to which she would allow herself to inhale any noxious smoke before deciding to take the plunge.

"Professor." She set her coffee down, decidedly. "I show that table to people for different reasons. Do you understand? To you, that day, I showed it because you seemed to have forgotten something, and I mistook you for—for—well, frankly, you seemed to be a little lost. I'm sorry. But you looked like—like—" She didn't finish.

"Go ahead. Say it," I demanded.

"Like a ghost carrying all his possessions."

"Really. That wasted-looking."

"I'm sorry." She seemed to be genuinely so. "I was only trying to explain."

"Sometimes explanations do more harm than good."

"I know. I've just realized what I've said."

"So wasted-looking."

"I was only trying to be accurate."

"It's quite all right. Some days we're not ourselves. Not at our best, I mean."

She didn't catch the criticism. "I know." She shook her head. "We all know that feeling."

It is strange to me how, sometimes, though very rarely, two people who hardly know each other at all, and who have almost nothing in common, and perhaps aren't even sure they like each other, or want to, will stumble instinctively and at the same moment across a narrow, treacherous, conversational isthmus, and arrive suddenly on a wider, more open plain. I looked at her. She was looking frankly at me.

"You know Dutch?" I sighed, relieved, suddenly struck by the naturalness of this question. "You could read the handwriting. Your accent was good."

"I studied languages when I was younger. Dutch, German, French, Czech. I was going to be a diplomat's aide. Do you still use a great deal of your first language?"

"No. Not really."

"I can tell. You have hardly the trace of an accent."

"I've been here so long."

We spoke of dialects, and of Europe. Of her intricate, bookcased desk, which, she explained to me, was Danish, not French. We talked of fine woods. Of overseas resources. Of cities we knew. Of architectural styles and forms. While, *Won't you sell that table to me? I* wanted, as we explored this new open range politely together, to shout out at her. *Perhaps since we are out here, out on this wide, safe veld, you will plainly see my needs, without my saying anything, and grant me my desire. Ah, Mrs., Ms., Cora Lowenstein!* I wanted to take her long hands in mine and persuade her. I wanted to get it all over with. *Please, please, do not make me explain, to lie to you, or tell you the truth, not now, do not make me reveal anything or apologize to you. I can't do it, it's not my place, and in any case I was only a boy, and now I am an old man, with a fly buzzing in my ear. Release me.*

"Mrs. Lowenstein, I don't have much time. . . ." It was nearly noon. The day was passing. I desperately needed a new approach.

"But we haven't even discussed your motif."

"No, no," I corrected her, shaking my head. "I mean— I'm nearly seventy years old. I don't know if I should be contemplating major changes. It's a strange feeling. There are just a few things, as you get older, that are important, that become precious, that you need to see to before you have to be—off." Wonderfully managed, I decided. Perhaps my age would work on her, begin to draw out her sympathy.

"Ah, well." She smiled. "You look too healthy today to be seventy. Look at you. You're like some ruddy soccer player, sitting there. Those cheeks."

You are an old fool. You can't even think decently, anymore, or plan ahead. You have never been able to see any farther than one cursed word in front of the other.

"Can't I interest you in one selection before you go?" she coaxed, businesslike again. "Perhaps—the harp chair you so admired last week? There is something so delightful about a new chair in the house. It makes you feel you have a new friend. It's really crucial, as we get older, to pursue fresh perspectives, wouldn't you say?"

"Now I see why you are such a success at this."

And here Cora Lasher Lowenstein colored. For the first time. Faintly. As though I had caught her laying a trap for me. As though her hands had not moved quickly enough away from her collaborators, those duplicitous French lying in wait outside her office door. She didn't seem to know, suddenly, what to do with her long, ringed fingers; they played with her coffee saucer, with the paperweights on her desk, turning them around by degrees, inch by inch, as if she were trying to reset a dial.

"I only know that good seating arrangements make the world a better place," she said stiffly, looking down. Her gray sweep of hair shaded her face for a moment. I thought she looked alone. Bereft among her trinkets. "I think chairs are central to good living, Professor Martens."

"Mrs. Lowenstein," I said breathlessly, for all at once I could see my way back to my original, bold idea. "May I take you for a short walk, and out to lunch?"

6

MOST MEN, given the chance to impress a woman, will not walk.

Most of us understand, instinctively, that standing on our own we don't amount to much, but that being accompanied by a moving vehicle, we borrow its fluency.

For example. A man standing next to a motorcycle sends out a message that he is capable and free. Adventurous—in the way of pirates. In his jacket and glasses, he is also vaguely reminiscent of a flying ace. But, too, he telegraphs to the world that he is grounded in pavement and dust, an intimate of both the cities and the backroads. He is the representative of life, of movement, of futurity. He is a consistent drone, confident, moving steadily away. Best of all, he is at the same time forever arrested in boyhood, immune to both failure and success. He is a distant figure of romance.

My mother first saw my father standing next to a motorcycle, one fine summer holiday while climbing as a tourist below the fairy-tale castle of Neuschwanstein.

She was just sixteen. Still a German country girl. Still persistent in her determination to see something of the world before she was forced to dig in her heels and begin tugging at the mule of life. There, in the valley below the floating, white-spired castle, she saw him. He held a box camera in his hands and wore shiny new binoculars around his neck. His white ears flared outward, startlingly, like Pegasus' wings. His dark hair was tousled. His pant legs were tucked into his awkwardly laced boots. He was gawky and handsome at the same time. Her heart beat, and she wondered what it would be like to talk to such a carefree, gangling, Dutch city-boy.

She began by asking him, in German, if she could borrow his glasses. Then, for permission to hold his camera and take a picture of him. (My sister and I later pored over this photo, amazed.) Soon she was asking his name and chattering to him, nattering, poking, flirting, circling him in such a way as to suggest they were both simply a pair of beautiful white swans teasing familiarly on the green lake below— when in fact she was pretending to be something she wasn't, and didn't know that he was doing the same. But then, it was always difficult to tell anything from my father's eyes, which were distant even at close range, and skittish, as though he had spotted something threatening him behind you.

In this manner my mother began her pursuit of my father. On that fine summer day, she had already imagined him rescuing her, throwing her up and carrying her away on his saddle. A prince on his movable kingdom.

Unaware that, in the end, he would be something rather more like *Gymnopholus lichenifer*, the walking-garden beetle, a species which carries with it an entire household on its back, without ever being aware of what is riding on it.

I ONLY LET MYSELF be talked into the wild extravagance of an eighteenth-century harp chair to lure Cora Lowenstein to come out of her shop with me, and because, moreover, I thought it would make me look more earnest in her eyes. After we had settled on a ridiculously high price, we left the building and strolled into Chelsea and took seats in a small, trendy café of her choosing. She smiled, politic, congratulating me again on my "bargain."

The waiter who refilled our glasses seemed to know her quite well. He didn't appear, in any case, to be at all put out while we lingered over soups at his best table. Immediately, this was of some concern to me. Was this woman, after all, in the habit of taking protracted lunch breaks to induce older, overwrought men to buy her *bibelots*? Did that waiter Emil, loitering there, stand to gain, somehow? I realized I was going to have to make myself more specific in Cora Lowenstein's thoughts. Less pedestrian. More tangible. And so I carefully worked my way around to talking about my heart troubles, and of my prolonged sorrows for my ex-wife.

"It's been almost ten years since we separated." I sighed and sat back from the table. "It took me three years, I think, just to get used to being alone again. I know it was for the best—that she had to tend to herself, for a while, after having looked after me for so long. She needed to pursue her spiritual health, alone. That's what she called it. Her 'spiritual health.' I only minded that she went looking for spiritual health so soon after my angioplasty." I heard myself sounding generous. Forgiving. I said nothing about how detached I'd felt when Agnes left me, like an astronaut floating in uninterrupted space. "I'm just not sure it's right to leave someone when they're down and out, you know. A person could at least wait until they're up and on their feet again."

"Yes. And did you have any children together?"

She had finished her crab bisque and was dabbing at her mouth, listening attentively. Her movements were graceful, fluid, unconscious, as though she was used to being well mannered even when no one was looking at her.

"Yes. I have a son. In Texas. Christopher. And I have a grandson, Ray. My ex-wife is also in Texas."

"Do you have any other family?"

"Not immediate. There might be a few more Martens, somewhere. It's difficult to know, at this point."

"Why is that?"

"Because my mother and father lost contact with what was left of their families after the war. It was a time of great upheaval and disturbance for all of us. Rotterdam was basically destroyed. Everything, everyone, had to start all over again." I was surprised at how natural, how normal my voice sounded as I said this. It might have been the soup. My throat felt smooth and relaxed. I felt calm inside, and the words coming out seemed common, not at all suspicious. I was simply having lunch with and talking to a Mrs. Lowenstein.

She continued to listen, looking clear-eyed across at me. Her ears were flushed and transparent in the light from the window beside us. The lobes looked like small glowing lanterns hanging from her. She had been having wine with her meal, which I try to avoid.

"So you have memories from the war," she prompted again, helpfully.

"Yes. And you?"

"Oh! I didn't think I looked old enough for that."

Another mistake. I apologized profusely. But she wasn't so easily offended.

"I've just turned fifty-three." She tilted her head and narrowed her eyes and turned the stem of her glass, adjusting again.

"And you . . ." I wasn't sure how to proceed. "Did you lose any family?"

"No. But my husband lost many, many of his cousins in Europe."

We both sat looking down at our empty soup bowls for a moment, at the scrapings at the bottom, abstract pieces of flesh.

"It's an odd thing," I went hurriedly on. "About that table that you have, up there. You said that people, after they've seen it, often want to buy your other things."

"I didn't say that. It all depends on the customer."

"But you don't think that it's . . ." I paused. What was essential here was to be restrained, and yet forceful. A wise, older man; one who respected the finer ethical points. "You don't think that it's perhaps a bit manipulative?"

"But that's not my intention. I don't want to keep it to myself. I don't want it to sit hidden away in my apartment."

"A museum didn't want it?"

"They say it can't be authenticated."

"But what do you think happens when someone reads those words and then turns around and buys the thing standing right next to it?"

She altered her position to study the people passing outside the window. They were hurrying, with heads aimed bulletlike against the wind. "I don't know. I think, in some cases, it's a way to reassure themselves. That it's all behind them. That they are safe now, and can go on and do what they like. Or maybe—and this is really what I hope it is—it's a way to be close to something that matters. Something beautiful and terrible, all at once. A way to stay in the room with that. To breathe the same air of something you feel a part of. Sometimes that's all you can do. Stand in the room and breathe with it." She went on looking out the window.

"Then you might be taking advantage of people's sensitivities."

"No." She turned back to me, adamant. "You're imagining that everyone who sees that table buys an entire suite. That isn't the case."

"But those who *do*," I persisted, my voice not quite so calm, not quite so normal now. "How do you know it isn't something else entirely?"

"For instance?"

"For instance, like guilt. They turn around and buy from you because you make them feel guilty. Or it's an appropriation. People trying to be part of something they know nothing about. Or self-righteousness. 'I am moved by this, I am unable to walk out of here without acting. Behold, I'm a person of action. Just look at me.' You see?"

"You've thought something about this, haven't you?"

Careful. She was looking narrowly at me again.

"I just don't think it's safe," I said, "to leave some things open to interpretation. You don't know what you might be inviting."

"I disagree. The idea is a simple one. *Als de Joden weg zijn is het onze beurt.* We are each implicated in the other's fate. That doesn't invite. It states. My husband, in any case"—she changed the subject and smiled slightly—"would have gotten into an argument with you. Sandor would have told you to mind your own business. He would have told you that when people spend good money for beauty and quality, the reasons are theirs alone, and the wise man is happy to make a profit."

"You said he was an amateur."

"Not where his livelihood was concerned."

"Still, no one could offer you enough money to sell something like that table—could they?"

"No. I couldn't sell it. It was his."

"But isn't what was his, now yours? You weren't divorced at the time of his—"

"No," she said sharply.

"But then—"

"That's not what I'm talking about. I'm only saying I'm not connected to it in *exactly* the same way he was. The distinction matters. It was his aunt's table. She was in hiding throughout the war. In Holland. You of all people must understand what that must have been like. The odds. She was given the table when she came out, and she brought it with her, and she left it when she died here, to Sandor. And since he has no more family, and we have no children, I'm passing it along, *this* way. In my own way."

She went on, telling me something of herself. She was half Jew-

ish. Born in Bridgeport. Her father was a gentile, descended from
Moravians originally by name Leshikar. His father—her grandfather—on landing at Ellis Island had changed the spelling of the family name to Lasher, to sound as American as possible. Her mother was
the daughter of an art dealer, who had also changed his name, although in his case to sound like a gentile. Her parents had met at a so-
cialists' gathering during the Depression.

"On my husband's side," she continued, matter-of-factly, "his
parents are no longer living. They were Jews born in Germany. He
was born here, but only because they fled Berlin in time. He doesn't
have any other immediate family. No brothers or sisters. So it's been
my responsibility, to think for him, to think what the Lowenstein
family would want. And then to think with my own history and conscience, as well. My own feelings. It isn't always easy, you know.
There's a feeling of uncertainty, sometimes . . . sometimes it's better
simply to put things out in the open. To place things, to leave them
out where there is potential, where they can be seen, and then owner-
ship, the decision of what belongs to whom, of what is what—I believe something else can take its place. Sometimes the best we can do
is to make sure we don't let go. Don't give in to our own sense of the
inevitable."

I nodded sympathetically, hoping she noticed the sincerity in my
looks. I wasn't exactly sure what she had meant by all of this—
though I felt I must have gotten the gist of it. More important, I had
glimpsed something, with anticipation, *possible,* something almost intimate, between us. She didn't continue, however, dropping her napkin on her plate with finality. And it was at this point that I dropped
my own elbow, trying for the same note of healthy conclusion, trying

to match my motions to hers, and shattered my soup bowl from the table.

THE SOUND OF IT hitting the polished concrete floor so startled me that for a moment all I could do was sit upright, hearing the echo of my last heartbeat fading away in my ears.

Everyone in the café was now staring at me.

"Don't worry," Cora Lowenstein said quickly, seeing my consternation. "Emil will take care of it."

"I'm so sorry. So sorry. So stupid."

"Not at all."

"I must have miscalculated—"

"Don't think of it."

"Such a mess."

"Not at all."

I was deeply, deeply mortified. Now, whatever intimacy I had glimpsed so briefly between us, scattered and lapsed. Now, she saw that I couldn't respond to something as simple as a cracked plate. That I panicked, like a child. Emil had signaled to a busboy, who was wiping the floor at my feet without looking up at me.

"I don't know what I was thinking—"

"Happens to me, sometimes. I forget I'm in a world with stupidly inanimate things."

"I'm not normally so obtuse. My vision is perfectly good."

"You're lucky then. Let's leave this, shall we? Everything seems to be under control."

"Allow me." I reached clumsily for my wallet.

"I won't hear of it." She waved my hand away. Slightly brusque. "You have no idea of my margin on your chair."

"Thank you for lunch, then."

"No. Thank *you*. It's been a long time since I've sat and talked so comfortably with anyone."

She was right. I had no ideas. None. I knew nothing, nothing, nothing, about anything. Except that I understood: I was being overcome by something—but what was it?—perhaps by something of that hunger other, unsuspecting customers had yielded to in Cora Lowenstein's elegant presence. Something in her steady glow. Because by now I was positively grateful that I would be taking a piece from her *milieu* home with me. I was eager, impatient even, to have any item of her furniture in my apartment. To sit with, to breathe in, to share the same air with—just as she had said. But it had nothing to do, I told myself wonderingly, with that curse of a table she kept in her shop. No. It was Cora Lowenstein herself who inspired this feeling. I noted this with complete clarity, and a little awe. It was her sternness, her evenhandedness, her deference. This woman—she made you feel as if there was still order to be found, that it circulated somewhere in her vicinity, that it could be subtracted from her, though she remained fixed and steady. She was so balanced. Almost frozen. Even as we walked back through the after-lunch crowd, she seemed to be still, in motion but somehow static, the effect again like the passing of a distant ship. In my anxiousness to understand and observe this, I became so absorbed in her, in looking at her, in walking beside her, as she strode with her head straight forward, chatting casually, her shawl tossed over her shoulder in a white mantle, I almost forgot I had meant to make her trust me only so that I could wrestle from her a prized possession.

And then there was this luck: she was only half Jewish. This was a further source of my surrender. I admit it. Not every atom of her being was necessarily, historically opposed to mine. I caught our reflection together, in profile in a florist's window, and for a moment saw us as a pair of nattering, married Long Islanders.

I left her at the entrance to the Chelsea Building. Only with the most stringent effort was I able to say good-bye, and touch my hat, and conceal my helpless attraction.

W HEN THE CHAIR ARRIVED at my apartment I stood looking excitedly down at it. The deliverymen, two tall jumpsuited fellows, began tearing the wrapping from its curved arms and legs
roughly. *Stop! For God's sake! Please,* I almost shouted. I wanted
them to move more slowly, deliberately. For the love of all that was
good! They were treating Cora Lowenstein's treasure as though
it were nothing more than a bale of hemp wrapped in banana
leaves.

When they'd finished, one of them handed me an invoice to sign
while the other squatted to sweep up a few pieces of bubbled plastic.
They both glanced into the hall-tree mirror before they left, adjusting
their braids. I thanked them and tipped them and hurried them out the
door, ecstatic to be left alone, at last, with the lush, strange smells in
my living room of varnish and mothballs and silk.

So. Here were beauty and quality, then.

As chairs went, it was certainly a lovely one. The woven back did
look something like a classical harp. Its curved arms ended in small

clusters of carved roses. Its feet were small and turned under, like an animal's at bay. The seat was broad and inviting.

But I didn't plan to sit down in it. I had informed Cora Lowenstein—honestly—that I considered the chair something of an investment. For several minutes all I wanted to do was stare at it, to think of her elegant, ringed fingers as they had stroked the back of it, to imagine how one exchange might lead to another, one piece to the next, and so on, and so on, and so on . . . to my ultimate goal at the end of the aisle.

Now, however, I had to face a question of a more immediate nature: Where was I going to put it? There, against the wall of the living room, beside my rumpled sofa, it looked ridiculous. Among all my things—my computer hardware and cables, my desk and floor piled high with books, my specimen drawers, my television, my scratched dining suite, my filing cabinets, my coffee table, my faded rugs—from all these things, the anomalous French chair drew itself apart, as if repelled. I carried it into the bedroom, but that was no good, either. I couldn't fit it beside my bed, or at the end of it. Panting, I carried it out and set it down again at the end of my kitchen cabinets. There it seemed to huddle, like a hostage. But not completely abject. In that corner, at least, it made a small statement of brightness.

I would be able to look at it while I ate my herring. I would be able to wheel around in my chair from my desk, and see it. When I paid my bills, or answered letters, or read my electronic messages, when the holiday cards and old fruitcakes from older colleagues began rolling in, as soon they would, and Elida Hernandez messaged that she wanted to come over and bring her mother's *pozole* for dinner and fret more about her research, and my son wrote to accuse me, again, of parental failure and neglect, I would be able to turn and look at the chair, and know that I had done something positive. I had taken steps.

One thing was certain. I would never never never, I told myself as I sank into the sofa, sit in and wear out such a ludicrously expensive piece of furniture. I would keep it unmarked. Unperforated. Unlike everything else in my apartment.

&

THE MOTORCYCLE my father had posed against that day, I should explain, hadn't been his.

It must have been the property of some other tourist, wandered off down below the castle of mad King Ludwig to urinate in his glassy, white-swanned lake.

Not until much later did my mother learn it was all a sham. That summer day, she had taken away with her only the image of a wealthy city boy staring all agog through his binoculars at a German castle, a foreign boy who had lent her his glasses and walked with her along the edge of the woods, and who had told her his name, and later the name of the street in Rotterdam where he lived—details my mother stuck like feathers into her cap.

By the time she was seventeen, she let it be known she wasn't going to marry and settle down on one of those overcrowded vineyards, and had decided she would go off and find work. Her parents, whose stands were at that time infested with beetles (and who had still another plain-looking daughter to marry off) agreed that she could hire herself out.

Perhaps they weren't cautious enough. Perhaps, like Agnes and me, they grew blank in the face of a child's strange will. Or perhaps they misread the signs. Perhaps, like us, they thought everything would turn out for the best.

It was decided, as wasn't at all unusual in those days for many healthy, stout, young German country girls, that she would go across the border into Holland and work as a maid.

My mother said she knew which city would suit her.

Her parents wrote to an older woman from the village who worked in the house of a wealthy Dutch Catholic family. She answered that she would try to get my mother a place. Soon they were helping her to pack and carting her off to the station and watching as she waved her handkerchief gladly back toward them. My mother was so excited she could hardly breathe or shout, she told us. When the train had passed beyond the last steeple, she felt exactly as if she had bitten it off and tried swallowing it whole.

I WOKE TO DISCOVER the creases in my face from the sofa cushion. I hadn't meant to doze. I could still feel the rumbling under my feet, hear the whistle, smell the bodies pressed close together in the car.

I put my hands on either side of my hips to steady myself. Such a headache. And my stomach. Time for the Pepto. I stood and walked cautiously over and groped above the kitchen sink and inside the cabinet, then went over to the window as I drank from the bottle, and blinked down onto the street. Somewhere, how far down exactly I couldn't be sure, the L-train roared on its tracks. All these years later. And the world still hung on to trains. In spite of all our advances, the Chunnel and the Shuttle, and a space station dangling over our heads like an unfinished crown. Yet still we managed a necessity for trains. The lumbering, incongruous, indisposable, thought-drowning things.

CHAPTER

9

IT WAS WHILE on a subway train that I steeled myself to read Christopher's early Christmas letter. This had been pumped like a series of rounds into my e-mail, the words bursting, intensely, leaving streaks like powder flashes on my computer screen. So much so that it hurt my eyes to look at them; that I had to print the letter up, on plain paper, and then send the original electronic message into the electronic garbage pail; for it is difficult to take so much intensity from a child, particularly from a grown child, difficult particularly through such an immediate link, where you can almost feel the sender at the other end, the sounds of typing, of hitting, of clicking, of the keys being pulled back—the angry writer removing the safety.

On such occasions, when I need a kind of distance, when I need the noise and tumult of the cars, I abandon whatever plans I've made for walking, and print up what he has written, and head down to the station.

I hadn't been able to reach Cora Lowenstein, in any case, since the brief, flattering phone call I'd made to her the week before to report my satisfaction with the harp chair. After that, I had decided it would be best to wait for another day or two (it was difficult to remember precisely how the rules of courtship went); yet when I'd tried to call again, with a question I'd fabricated about a slight fog on the varnish, I was told by her assistant she had gone on a buying trip and would be away indefinitely.

"You don't know when she'll be back?"

"It varies with the interest."

I took this as a poor sign, and a significant one. She hadn't even mentioned this absence to me during our phone conversation. Had never even hinted she would be unavailable. I gave myself over to brooding, pessimistic thoughts about my tendency toward mistakes and mishandlings. And then, my son's Christmas letter had arrived. With cruel timing. So now I rode thoughtlessly, changing lines occasionally, without any fixed destination, frowning and shuffling in the press and company of coated and mud-splattered strangers who, even though this was New York City in winter, might, I hoped, notice if I collapsed to the wet newspapered floor from a fatal heart attack brought on, in the end, by the sheer unmitigatedness of my son's rage at and disapproval of me.

I KNOW THAT, at thirty-eight, he still holds me responsible for his addictions and failures. He once told me—all right, I'll admit this was fairly well put—that I was like the priest who, having learned his religion was wrong, locked the doors to every building with a pointed roof.

He's still just a boy, I thought stubbornly as I clung to the metal rail overhead—just a boy, and a confused one, at that. I felt better when I was able to grab a seat facing the sliding doors. *He is just a boy taking aim at a father who has, so far, refused to return his volleys.* I am aware that my son is a warlike Christian who collects firearms and prays to Jesus for the strength to defend himself against the forces of darkness. My understanding (from his mother) is that he owns several rifles and pistols and Uzis down there in Texas, and is thoroughly equipped to protect his mother and wife and son, and his gated, barred, suburban one-story brick home, from enemies he has not yet clearly named, and at which I am afraid to guess.

There are certain species of New Guinean fly (*Phytalmia alcicornis*) who war with one another by slashing with a pair of unusual, armored, spearlike protuberances they brandish from just below their widely separated eyes. All this thrashing and stabbing at one another is perfectly normal, and probably builds endurance for their battles against other opponents. But sometimes, through genetic mutation, or unpredictable and unchecked growth, one fly's spear extends and hardens and becomes too long and too heavy. And he drops, finally, underneath it, incapacitated by the very adaptation designed to protect him. All he can do then is wiggle his legs, unable to move, living in dread of the scavenger ants ready to come along and carry him away.

This was the letter my son sent to me:

Dear Father

Well. I hope this message finds you well, and taking better care of yourself. I can't tell you how much it would mean to all of us if you would turn to your spiritual health, as well as your physical well-being, at this approaching time of year, and come to the glory of Jesus Christ, who will wait for you with open arms at the season of his birth, as well as at all other seasons.

You know that I can never let this time of year pass without hoping for that. You know that it isn't too late—it is never too late to come to the Lord. Mama has done it, and every day for her, as it is for all of us, is now a welcome and a rejoicing and a celebration. We are all here, and YOU the only one who is absent. If I can forgive in you what has been in my opinion a whole lifetime of EMOTIONAL ABSENCE FROM YOUR FAMILY, and from the Lord, surely you should have enough strength now to admit you need Him, in your suffering, and need us, and come down here, and lift yourself up to HIM.

I don't have to remind you that it was because of you that I had for so many years a vacuum in my life that I treated with drink and medicated with drugs, because you didn't see the way to fill our lives with the light and comfort and food of spiritual salvation. When I think of how lonely I felt. When I think of how I tried so pointlessly to be the things you wanted me to be. I have never understood the GODLESSNESS AND FAITHLESSNESS of our house during those years; why you set your face so firmly against the pathways of Our Lord Jesus Christ, Savior. If I had only had some direction, some knowledge of a Supreme Authority, and a sense of my own place and servitude in His army, I would not have gone astray in the ways that I did. It would not have taken me so long to become a man, and a husband, and a father, and a successful business owner. So long to acknowledge my own sins and helplessness in this world, and give myself over to the CHRIST inside Christopher.

When I think back on those times and the coldness and emptiness of our lives, I wonder that we didn't perish without the light. It is a sin and a curse to tell a child that the world is a Godless place, a machine made of happenings and hard matter. You were blind, Papa. You shut us out of the Kingdom of Heaven, me and Mama both, and she sees it now, too. She cries and cries and cries when she thinks of how she almost left this life without seeing the face and comfort of the Lord before her, doomed instead to eternal Hell and wandering. How could anyone want that for someone they love? She still cries and cries, worrying about your immortal soul. We all do. I know we could never be a family again in the same way that we were before she left you—Mama has accepted that as your sin and her weakness—but we could all be children of the Lord together, couldn't we? A family of God, of servants. I am ready to show you the way. Can't you see how much better it would be, all of us here together, singing His praises, trusting something higher, something great, to watch over us and forge us as one into shining armor? What do you have, out there, sitting alone with your microscopes and cockroaches?

We are your only family. Who else will comfort you? NO ONE. This has never been a spiritual family, until now. If it had been, if only God had been allowed in the room with us, we wouldn't have lost our way among the Pharisees and unbelievers and importers of perversion. I have reclaimed the name of this family for Christ. There is neither shame nor fear in loving the Lord. The time has come—and not a minute too soon. Any day, any minute now the hand of God could fall across you—and would you be ready? Would you be willing to leave this world without seeing your grandson?

Only come to us now and all will fall away like ashes from the mound. I am ready to help you. Come and wash yourself clean in His wounds. We love you very much. We thank you, as always, for your generous check, which goes into Ray's home-schooling fund. Not an hour goes by that Betsy and I, and Mama too, don't wish you were here with us, that you would take one step of a thousand miles and begin to meet salvation with a smile of victory on your face. Until that time, you know we don't feel it would be right for you to see Ray. He is so young. He might learn too much from you, understand too much.

I wish you the peace of God Eternal and Everlasting, and hope you will finally answer not me, but HIM, through which all hope for the future flows.

Your loving family,
Chris, Betsy, and Ray (and Mama)

I stared down at the last sheet of paper, curling like a scroll over my fingers. The effect of this letter on me was much the same as that of all the others I have been periodically bombarded with in recent years. I felt for a moment a little surreal—as though I had reached down to pick up something as simple and reliable as a stone, and pulled up instead a severed calf's head. I folded the pages away and stuck them in my coat, and then looked down at my palms resting on my knees. My fingers wriggled and jerked, uncomfortably. It takes a minute, always, for my circulation to come back; for the realization of my only child to sink in, for me to absorb the kind of man he has become, and swallow it, and then straighten. The older woman sitting next to me, wearing a hard-looking hat, a helmet in the shape of an igloo, looked over my knuckles as well.

"Arthritis is awful," she leaned over and said in a Brooklyn drawl. "Some days I feels so bad it seem like it can't be me."

I nodded, without correcting her.

A young couple, hanging on to the rail over our heads and with their free arms wrapped around each other's necks, looked down as though I and my seatmate were prehistoric, as though a pane of glass separated our decrepit, museumlike world from theirs. They turned away, chewing something.

More than once it had occurred to me that I should overcome my disgust and disappointment and answer his letters. *Dear Christopher. Let us begin by drawing clearer distinctions. Though they are both industrious insects, and part of the web of life, a cockroach is not a beetle.* But that would take energy, and I was tired. Time, when I had other projects at hand. I had been through so much already. Better, I thought glumly, simply to let things ride, for now. He couldn't be, in spite of his guns, a dangerous boy, could he? Most of the damage he had done he had done to himself. And since it was too painful to think of my grandson, too distressing to imagine his tiny, impressionable frame, I shut the thought of his likely education out, and rubbed my gouty knee with my hand and listened to the thumping of the rails.

I didn't want, at that moment, to be the particular father of a particular son. I wanted to be the opaque reflection in the young couple's distant eyes. Or the counterpart to the swollen wrists of the hard-hatted woman from Brooklyn nodding off next to my shoulder. Or the echo of turns and bumps and brakings already taken by the three identical cars ahead of us. At the next station the young couple got off and were replaced by a group of wool-capped thugs even younger. They didn't notice me, but blocked my view of the doors, closing me in like a pack of jackals. For a moment I felt wonderfully passive, a body within a larger body, hurtling via electromagnetic compulsion through space.

MY SON IS RIGHT in one respect, at least. I have been alone. But not more alone, after all, than at other points in my life. As a young faculty member with a young wife, I rarely felt more solitary than at a showy, noisy, stiff-backed academic function, when I stood with a drink in my hands, my second, or third, or fourth, or fifth, swaying in the middle of a sea of plush red carpet, wondering how it was that I had managed to fool them all, how I had scuttled my way into a world of deans out of the riffraff and ruin of my family. With Agnes in my arms afterwards, making love to her, trying to blot out the seeping agony of an evening, I was still alone, apart, drunk with disbelief, as she must have understood and felt and resented.

Poor Agnes. Thirty years of being the dutiful academic wife. Thirty years of enduring my long disappearances into the jungles and mountains, and then, even when I was at home again, of withstanding inside the walls of our white two-story house my bad-tempered re-fusals and unexplained detours around the corners of memory. Of course, I never told her what I had emerged from. I never told any-

one. Certainly not American Agnes. So that finally, having grown
weak and stiff like a limb forced to hold in one position for too long,
she broke cleanly away from me. Of course, I understand that. Of
course I know the blame is partially, maybe completely, mine.

We used to tell everyone, Agnes and I, that we met while skiing in
Vermont. *What a good story!* People laughed when we told them how
we had crashed into each other on a hillside because we had both been
so clumsy and inexpert and nervous. *Oh yes, you should have seen us, it
was hilarious. It was fate bringing us together.* But that wasn't how it
happened at all.

Agnes had almost struck a tree, only narrowly escaping killing
herself. She lay in the snow on her back, in the lengthening shadows,
crying. I came along and nearly skied over her in the dusky light. But
I managed to stop, and look down, and there she was, tear-stained and
red-cheeked and cloudy-breathed. She couldn't have been more
American-looking, more wholesome, more fresh-apple-pie-ish, had
I picked her out of a *Saturday Evening Post.* She told me her name,
and then I sat down next to her, and asked if she was all right, or
needed help. And then, in a rush it had all come out. How she had
been skiing blindly and recklessly because her fiancé from college had
just dumped her, and for his hometown sweetheart, no less. How
she'd thought she could get over it, thought she just would go on a
holiday, anyway, and recover—but obviously she couldn't do it—
she—she—she had just—or nearly just—oh, God! And then she had
cried and cried. Later, when we were married, she was no longer so
quick to let her emotions out. Though whenever she did, it was like
watching one of those Christmas carousels spun wildly by the flames
underneath it.

She was only twenty-two and I was only thirty and foreign and nervous and accented, and still a year shy of my Ph.D. But she was pretty. And awkward. I felt the same surge of pity toward her as I did for a pillbug struggling on its back. I believe that, at that time, I was incapable of distinguishing between a pillbug and a human being. A grave error. I can only say, in my defense, that at that point in my life I was still experiencing difficulty recognizing human beings at all.

And then later you came along, Christopher, and were from the first a strange child, a road without a map, a boat without a rudder, and all my attempts—our attempts—to give you direction, skills, talents, horseback riding or sailing or wood shop or music lessons, to find something that would fix you, help you, never worked, never worked, and I don't know why—unless it was that I was afraid to see the restlessness in your eyes for what it was. I saw eventually of course that all my coaxing and tempting and bribing you was a bad idea. I thought I could give you an objective framework, a series of clear, safe steps, an outline so hospitable you would lose your formlessness in it, and become a man (or at least, like me, a being bearing the outward shape of a man). I was younger then. I thought things would be easier, for you. That everything was possible, in this country. I didn't anticipate your tunnel, your spiral. If only I could have apologized for it, I would have.

But how does one apologize for being a failure? When it's so pointless, so redundant. When might a human being reasonably be allowed to forgo "I'm sorry," and say only to another human being, leaping past apology like an arrow: "Forgive me, I loved you"?

I L O O K E D A R O U N D T H E T R A I N and wondered if my lips had been moving. Lately I have begun to worry about signs of incipient senility. I've developed the occasional tic, I know, of thinking out loud. I glanced right and left, embarrassed. But of course no one would have paid attention, even had I been yelling at the top of my lungs.

The car was now nearly empty. It was getting late and the few people riding with me in it were nodding in their seats, all of us, together, nearly comatose with the effort of balancing the heavy bulbs of our brains on the stems of our necks. My own shoulders and neck were hurting from sitting and bowing my head for so long. I would get off at the next stop, whichever it was. And walk. The familiar need to move asserted itself. I had to feel the ball of the earth turning impervious underneath me. I stood up and hung on to the handle beside the doors.

As always, when I'm about to pass in or out of a train, my heart fluttered briefly. I calmed it by reminding myself that my son was basically a good boy; that he had his own business now, designing computer games (I tried to overlook the fact that these apparently all involved guns and the slaying of long-chinned, long-nosed, red-eyed demons); that he was clean and sober and putting food on the table for my grandson; that Agnes was there and, though fallen under the same apocalyptic spell as the rest of them, at least could be counted on to be practical and safe, level-headed, a woman who knew enough to drive her husband to the hospital the first time he had complained of indigestion and his left arm going numb. And so I was able, by concentrating this way, to return my son to his life, where he belonged, in faraway Texas, just as the doors in front of me opened and a rush of air blasted me that was cold but better than the stale, recirculated carbon dioxide I had for the last several hours been breathing.

I stepped out onto the platform and turning noticed a small crowd gathered at the head of the train and looking down into the well of the tracks. The doors behind me didn't close, as they should have. They stayed apart, pulsing slightly back and forth, breathing mechanically. The people at the head of the tracks were shouting and pointing down. Probably some old man like myself had just been pushed or fallen. Since I wasn't in a hurry I decided to go forward and see. What else was there to do?

I had given up calling and checking in at Lowenstein's Fine Antiques, irritated by the bored assistant's voice at the other end, telling me each time that Ms. Lowenstein was still traveling, that she had extended her trip, that she had gone to Nice, to London, that I could leave a message and she would return my call—or perhaps he could assist me with my design concept, if I could explain the concept? No, I wasn't sure I could explain the concept.

I drew closer and lifted my chin into a space above the shoulders of the turbaned man ahead of me.

"What is it?" I said.

"There! A lady's poodle has run down and got on the tracks."

The crowd was swelling now like a swarm, growing angry, angrier. Evidently the train had been about to run over the unoffending poodle. A young woman with a backpack—not, I guessed, the owner of the dog—was beating her tattooed fists against the bulletproof glass that protected the driver.

"You wait a fucking minute until someone gets that fucking dog, you heartless motherfucker! Aw, man, it's getting closer to the rail!"

I craned. I strained forward. Even though I really didn't want to look, because looking would be horrible. Yet I knew, knew if anything from my years in the jungle, from staring down into the trap of a pitcher plant while a spider crawled guiltlessly along its rim, that to look away, to walk away, was the even deeper cowardice and cruelty toward any small, helpless creature so near death. So I leaned forward into the crowd and caught sight of the poodle—I don't like poodles, particularly white poodles, particularly white poodles with their heads and ears cut to look like wedding cakes—and felt the blood that had so recently calmed and ordered itself inside me rush up again flushing into my head and chest. Because the little dog was tapping the red glints of its painted toenails foolishly, dangerously, back and forth, back and forth, closer and closer to the electrified rail. Looking up into the crowd, prancing and smiling. Closer still. No one was moving. Closer still. What an idiotic animal.

I couldn't stand it anymore. Wasn't anyone going to—?

"Look!" the backpacker shouted.

But I was just about to—

But it was too late. A burly member of one of the city's finest had arrived. He was down the laddered side of the tunnel in a flash, and now he tiptoed down into the oil and muck and yanked the white fur ball by its scruff. He scrambled up again, half frowning and half smiling, to the sound of applause and shouts of approval, while the little dog flashed its pink tongue, back and forth, back and forth, panting excitedly. As if all this ruckus and danger and risk were worth it. As if everything, everything were worth it, just to be brought up and feel yourself hugged tightly against a burly chest.

And then all at once I saw Cora Lowenstein step forward and hold her long, ringed hands out, and the dog was delivered over to her.

THE CROWD FELL AWAY from her the way people will when a mistake has been corrected and there is nothing left to do. Cora thanked the muscled officer, and then turned with the tufted dog in her arms, and saw me. I was so surprised and happy to see her again I could feel my mouth hanging on its hinges. Her eyes widened, in recognition. For a moment I was completely carried away by the familiarity in her look. Then it occurred to me that Cora Lowenstein might be remembering the restaurant, and the soup bowl, and putting two and two together, and realizing that I would always be present, but inevitably useless, on occasions of small crisis.

I transferred my attention to her dog, which I could see had suffered some smudges, and now that I was closer appeared to have been inexpertly groomed.

"My! Well!" I tried to sound hearty. "Look at this. Is he—she—it—all right?"

"I think so." She lifted the dog's head and scratched behind its ears. "Yes, he's fine. Just a little wanderlust, I'm afraid. Cooped up too much while I was away. Though I've never had anything like this happen before. He just slipped out of the collar and ran down here. Bad boy." She took a leash from her coat and pulled the yoke of a black leather collar around the poodle's neck, and set him at her feet. The collar had a silver bell attached. It jingled insanely as the dog shook its head back into place.

"What's his name?"

"Rumford. Rumford the Third. Good boy."

The poodle tripped to the end of his leash and stood looking around bright-eyed. Cora Lowenstein looked down at him, tolerant, unfazed. I knew that stance. She stood there unconsciously commanding, the scarf wound around her neck bringing out the color in her cheeks, her hair curled slightly at the temples, damp. She had been perspiring. Had she run down the station stairwell behind him? What would it tell me, what would I know about her, if she had? She whispered something in French to Rumford and nodded and looked up, and her face was very much settled now, having concluded some private matter between them.

"You've been away," I said. "I tried to call." I worried that this sounded too forward, so I added: "It was nothing that couldn't wait."

"I've been off on a buying expedition. Duty called." She gave a tug to Rumford's leash as he gravitated toward my shoes. "Do you live near here?"

So she didn't remember the delivery address. "No. You?"

"Just a block up."

"I got out and then I heard all the noise about helping someone."

She tilted her head to the side, her characteristic gesture. "Madness. What's the city coming to?"

I looked down at a torn piece of newspaper clinging to her calf. She was unaware of it. It leafed away.

"It's good to see you," I said, unable to help myself.

And here I'm forced to state: I am convinced I can't trust my own reflexes, anymore. In truth, I have become an old man. My eyes are not as quick as they once were, my hearing is selective, even my sense of touch, my fingers and toes and joints, behave in ways that are at times unaccountable to me. So it is with a certain degree of doubt that I now claim I saw, on that cold afternoon, a bit of fluster around Cora Lowenstein's mouth. Her lips looked suddenly as if they didn't know quite what they wanted to say. My own twitched uncomfortably, like clumsy, mating creatures that had landed on my face. The ordinary life of the station flowed around us; the gust from a passing line of cars blew by and almost knocked us backwards.

Rumford barked. It was more like a chirping.

"Suppose I should get him out of here," she brought out.

"Yes."

"It's so cold out today. I should have had his sweater on. I never remember, and of course it's my responsibility now. He could have just been running around to keep warm. So I ought to— Professor Martens, would you like to come up for a little coffee? Or is it tea? I'm close by. Only if it's convenient, of course. I don't know what your calendar's like."

"It would be a pleasure," I said. "I just happen to have some free time."

"Good."

I followed her and Rumford up the slick stairs and into the street. I was hopeful again. I admit it. She was beginning to trust me. There was a chance, a real chance for me, with her.

I ALWAYS FEEL FOOLISH when someone's home surprises me. It's as if you've been drawn a picture of your own limitations.

I was dumbfounded. I'd expected something completely different. I stood in her bare, lofted entry and took off my coat and muffler in something like a daze. Cora Lowenstein's apartment bore almost no resemblance to her store. It wasn't at all cluttered with fragile and cracked and overstuffed provincial things. The wide room she led me into, after taking my things from me, was almost Japanese in its simplicity. I caught pieces of my reflection in a large, lacquered coffee table, in the sleek black arms of the chairs, in the fat, balled feet of the deep paisley sofa she pointed me to. Over all of this, in the high ceiling, hovered a great, beamed, pyramid of space. Cora Lowenstein, it seemed, liked to keep a cone of air floating above her.

She invited me to sit and said she would be back with coffee. But I didn't sit. I had to examine, research. To prepare myself, study her background. Her walls were not, on closer inspection, papered, but washed with a kind of thick burnt orange paint, dark and warm. Metal light sconces were attached at even intervals around the room. The fronds of an exotic potted palm stood up and over me. I had the confused sense, as I turned around, that I was in a desert. In the corner stood a grand piano covered in a simple shawl, and on top of this a cluster of framed photographs.

Overall, I was disappointed. This was a formal room. A sort of salon. There was little to probe and gauge. This was a place for entertaining, for detouring visitors away from private and personal and disheveled spaces—or maybe it was to keep disheveled guests separate from even more pristine rooms? I brushed the wrinkles around the pockets and fly of my pants. She had proffered, after all, no great intimacy in inviting me here. She was simply being polite. She'd probably felt put on the spot by an older client—an odd, by now somewhat familiar man, who had twice visited her store, and who today had stood unexpectedly in front of her, in the subway station, looking wrinkled and befuddled and out of sorts, probably, after three hours of sitting on a train, and as though he needed a good warming.

She was making glassy noises somewhere, in the kitchen. I could hear Rumford's bell tinkling indistinctly down a hallway.

I walked in a circle and tried to make believe I was comfortable. There was no sign of the holiday in her apartment, at least. Neither menorah nor Christmas tree. Perhaps here, in any case, we had something in common. I hesitated and then walked over to the piano. It gleamed like a casket. I bent and put my nose closer to some of the picture frames. A younger Cora. Posed beside a man with windswept hair, like hers, and a lean and powerful build like an athlete's. They were leaning against a sports car; that looked like a beach lacing behind them.

"My husband," I heard her voice say directly behind me.

I straightened swiftly. Deliberately acting—I don't know why—as though I had been caught doing something I shouldn't have.

She stood there with the lacquered tray in her hands, looking past me.

"My hair was longer then. And darker." She smiled. And moved smoothly toward the coffee table. "And Sandor was so thin. He picked up a few pounds, later. Which was all right, he needed to."

"You have a beautiful place." I sat down on the sofa. "It's not what I imagined."

"What did you imagine?"

"You have widely ranging tastes."

"I never let San bring his businesses in here. I told him, I have to have a house that doesn't feel like inventory."

"So, it's always been like this?"

"For the last ten years or so, yes. I haven't gone to the trouble of changing anything important." She sat in an armchair and looked around, assessing. "Yes, it's all just the same. Sometimes I think people make too much of updating. It shows a lack of commitment, in my mind. I think you're a wise man, for instance. You simply start with one piece. A chair. Then you wait. You see if it grows on you. If it doesn't, you haven't made a mistake. If it does, you consider the next step. It's like building a phrase. And once you've got it right, you have to have faith. You can't pay attention to every *frisson* in the market."

"So what is truly beautiful and balanced endures, and demands loyalty?"

"Exactly. At least it should, in my opinion. You haven't had any regrets about your purchase?"

"No, no, no. The chair suits me perfectly. But your things here— are—are these your taste, or—or your husband's?"

"Both," she said shortly. "Which is one reason I don't change it."

This didn't bode well. Cora Lowenstein, obviously, clung to what was hers. I looked from under my brows at her. Nervous. But then, suddenly, nothing seemed to matter. Everything was quite casual, the way she managed it. She sat in the deep chair across from me. She poured coffee. She gave me sugar. She smiled her tolerant, elegant, widow's smile. I smiled back. It was like being too tired to argue at the end of a long day.

"How was your buying expedition?" I asked her.

"Productive. I found some beautiful things, outside Lyons. And then there's always a hungry elitist or two, needing some quick cash. Everything should arrive in about a month."

"I'll have to come and see the new shipments."

"I think you'll be pleased. And how have you been? Do you spend any time, these days, at the university?"

"Not much. I have one student in particular I'm still guiding. Who needs my attention. Once I'm finished with that, I'll be completely left to my own devices." Would she take the hint?

"I suppose that's nice, but for myself, retirement would leave me with too much time on my hands. Do you still do research?"

"A little."

"It was spiders, I remember?"

"No." I tried not to sound acid. "Beetles."

"That's right. I remember now. And look, I'm even wearing my scarab ring today, from Cairo. Sandor bought it for me there." She balled her fingers and reached her hand across the coffee table, so that I could see. I nodded, unsure whether to extend and touch it. The workmanship was excellent. The stylized *elytra* nestled in a shield around her middle finger.

"Beetles are magnificent," she said, sitting back.

"Thank you."

"Why did you decide to concentrate on them?"

"I like them."

"Such a simple reason. What should I know about them that I don't know?"

I looked up into her high, peaked ceiling and flipped through my mental drawer of stock answers. I didn't really want to talk about work. Let it be finished, set aside, left in other, more capable hands.

Let Elida Hernandez carry the torch for coleoptery. But still, some tidbits might, who knew, help me seem more exotic in Mrs. Lowenstein's eyes. So I puzzled over which facts might entice her.

Should I tell her that some beetles bury dead animals for food storage, mummifying corpses as large as birds and mice?

Or that beetles were once—unjustly—accused of landing on rooftops and starting fires?

Perhaps some etymology. "Beetle," from the Old English *bitula*, little biter; or "weevil," from the German *Webila*, meaning movement back and forth, teeming.

Ladybugs were once dedicated to the Virgin Mary. Dung beetles associated with sin. Scarabs roll balls of dung into masses the size of tennis balls, then guard their families meticulously inside them. Coroners and forensic anthropologists often put badly decomposed murder victims into their "bug boxes"—Plexiglas tanks filled with flesh-eating dermestids, which obligingly chew and leave nothing behind but the clean evidence of stripped bone. Beetles are the janitors of the planet. Without them, Wilson has written (but then, he was always something of a showboater), the world would be piled high with mounds of unconsumed, immobile, inabsorbable waste. And we would be overcome by our own existences.

"Most people"—I settled on a less unsavory example—"don't realize that it was his love of beetles that led Darwin to give up his studies to be a minister."

"So we can thank them for the Theory of Natural Selection?"

"I meant, for not making Darwin a priest."

"But he almost is one, isn't he?"

"You're not a Darwinian then."

"I think I am. But you'll have to admit terrible things can be done with good ideas. Or maybe it's that simple ideas can be made too simple. Don't frown." She smiled. "I'm all for science. In its more benign aspects. Sugar again?"

"Thank you."

I wanted to say to her: You handle the surface of things so well, Mrs. Lowenstein. Look at you. You are so effortless. So evenly keeled. So balanced. So poised. Whereas I, for example, at this very moment, feel as though I could slip on the sheen of all this lacquer and polish and land in a heap on the floor at your feet. You would no doubt very collectedly pick up your cell phone and dial 911. You would administer CPR and break a slight sweat from the strain. Your hair curling more tightly, more beautifully at the temples. Perhaps I don't really feel drawn to you, after all. Perhaps you are not quite human enough, for me. Perhaps I don't really want anything from you but that table, my table, the one you absolutely refuse to part with. You think you know what you're doing. But you don't. Maybe you are so balanced because nothing has ever rocked you.

"Where is Rumford?"

"I've locked him up in a bedroom. I've slipcovered the furniture in there. He can be a bit of a mess."

"I guess he's only a puppy."

"No—he's nineteen. Poodles are like that. Ageless. He was Sandor's dog. I try to take care of him as well as I can, to keep his spirits up. But it's not really my forte. I was never very good with small animals." She sipped her coffee. I could hear a faint clicking, squeaking sound at the back of her throat. Like a clarinet's reed, I thought. Feeling myself yearn toward her. I couldn't help myself.

"I don't see any children." I gestured toward the photos.

"We never wanted any."

"Why not? If it isn't too rude to ask."

"Of course it isn't. Any number of reasons. Sandor didn't trust the world enough, for one thing. You can hardly blame him. He told me he thought it was too burdensome, now, putting the state of the planet in a young person's hands. But then he felt guilty, because as a Jew he felt the future lay in numbers. And then I think"—she tilted her head—"he experienced a transference in the area of French poodles. We've had a succession of them. There are pictures over there of Rumford the First, and the Second."

"And your own reasons?"

"For not having children? Very selfish. I come from a large family, five younger brothers and sisters. I was the oldest. A crush of people, growing up. We were always fighting over something."

"I had only one sibling, myself."

"How lucky for you."

"Her name was Isolde."

"Tristan and Isolde? Your parents must have been Wagnerians!"

"I don't know."

"Then they must have been Romantics."

"Oh, no. Only my mother."

We sat for a moment in a lagoon of silence I found myself grateful for, staring out over my lifted coffee cup. I wondered how long I could go on this way. Sitting in this high, airy, dusky flat of Cora Lowenstein's, with a desert palm swaying over my head, and her late husband looking over my shoulder, his round eyes behind his round glasses staring out at me like a pair of loaded binoculars, his poodle locked up in a room somewhere because of me, ringing its bell feverishly. And there his piano, standing silently, which he must have played to his guests, or perhaps sometimes only to his wife, alone.

Would it have been Chopin? Schubert? Liszt? While she listened, right there, in that very seat, soaking in the expert vibrations of his lean, accomplished hands. And I was yearning toward her. While I sat huddled, unable to be truthful with her, to tell her that my mother was not romantic at all, no, no, by the time I knew her, but only rigid, and matter-of-fact, and grinding, and cold. I could smell myself sweating and suffering again. I began to look for a way to steer our meeting back toward my goal. For Cora Lowenstein must give in to me, Cora Lowenstein *must* see how badly I needed to pull my family's thorn from her side. And since I couldn't be honest with her in one way, I decided that the best thing would be to be honest with her in another, and let her see how pitiable I was. Let her see how needy and hungry an older man could really be.

"I do have my son. Christopher. But we don't speak."

"That's too bad. Was it because of the divorce?"

"No, Cora." There. I had used her name.

She blinked. Glancing away. Wiping the rim of her saucer with her napkin. She had spilled some cream. I'd noticed it. It then occurred to me, for the first time, that perhaps she sneezed as well. And brushed her teeth. And slept. And even hiccupped. Even more surprising to me, she leaned forward, and in a movement I hadn't seen before set her cup down and brought her knees together under her skirt with her hands, as though to prevent her legs from getting up and starting away. She sat very still. As though she wasn't sure she ought to listen.

OUT IT ALL CAME, all the mistakes I had ever made with my son, all the worry and trouble and ache that have continued for so many years, unending, unbroken—these were all still present to me even as I sat in Cora Lowenstein's vaulted living room, so present they seemed to have power enough to darken her curtains in front of me. Though a part of me knew it must be only that the day was so short. One of the shortest in the year, in fact.

I told Cora how, when Christopher was just a boy, we had despaired over his habit of killing small animals. How Agnes and I would open our freezer to find, at first, only tiny pollywogs frozen in pond water sealed in a Tupperware container. Then, later, several specimens of dead garden frog. Then later, larger lizards. Then baby white mice huddled in a frosted mass still in the shoebox nest in which he had found them. Then a chipmunk balled and covering its eyes and nose with its paws, its tail frozen and sticking in black plumes to the cubes in our ice tray.

We sent him to counseling. We put a lock on the freezer, and enrolled him in music lessons. In trumpet. We listened hopefully to the noises coming from behind his closed door as he tried to find the scale, his breath pushing and squeezing notes out like mud through a pipe. At least, we thought, this will exhaust him. At least, we hoped, he'll make friends now in the school band, and not be such a lone wolf; and he'll come to see the beauty in things, in living things, in art, and music, and poetry, and a world that could be as easy and open to him as the sun. But my boy couldn't read or spell well, at first. He had trouble with the haiku he was assigned,

See the mud cracking
After rain it drys up up
It bends up up up

and failed miserably at every sport.

But these were only the stumblings, we told ourselves, of a sensitive, normal kid who simply had to find his feet. And I had believed this until I found him, one day after school, when he was just fifteen, standing in the garage with a wad of bloody hair in his hands. Standing there, in our clean, shelved, three-car garage, with a bleeding wad of his own hair in his hand, a chunk from his own scalp the size of a small nest. And I had shouted and wept at him, stomping and cursing and asking, Why, why, why have you done such a thing?

To see if I could stand it, he said.

No surprise, later, that he was an indifferent college student. Or that he was unable to keep any of his part-time jobs, or that he drifted into bad company, into torn clothing, tattoos, alcohol, drugs—or that I, terrified, desperate, had to promise him that, if only he would finish his education and remain sober, I would pay to send him for a year to Alaska. From out of thin air it seemed to have come to him—this dream of going to Alaska. Something he longed for inexplicably, sobbing at night in his room as though blank fields of snow were the only surface he could imagine to cool the coals under his feet.

Then, as mysteriously as this wish had come, it vanished. And for a time, he had actually seemed to listen to me again. He had studied hard, and graduated decently, and was accepted into law school (though not without a great deal of academic string-pulling on my part), and we had believed, Agnes and I, that here, here at last, he would find a purpose, here he would be completely consumed. How his eyes had lit up when I told him that, now, he would learn to defend himself, how to *think*, intricately and complexly. How sure I had been that I was acting in his best interests. I even pointed out to him that I'd never expected him, as he once thought, to follow me into a scientific field; that this was all his, entirely his, new, and that we were so proud of him, our only son, our boy, who'd pulled himself up by his bootstraps.

And then, a year later, he simply dropped out of law classes and disappeared without a sign. It would be like that, again and again, for the next eight years. Christopher appearing and disappearing. Christopher turning up every so often in a jail cell or a rehabilitation center in California or Florida. Calling us and needing money. I hadn't even known where he was while the doctors in Houston were clipping the vein from my leg and knotting it around my heart. He didn't even call after the bypasses were complete. No, Christopher found his way to Texas much later, with a band of evangelicals he met while standing in a soup line at an Oklahoma City shelter.

"Christopher says I kept Jesus from him."

"What does that mean?" Cora pushed the tray and things awkwardly to one side, so that nothing lay between us now but the smooth plane of the coffee table.

My voice strained. I hadn't spoken so much, not in a long time. I had to clear my throat to keep it from tightening. I didn't want to sound inchoate in front of her.

"I'm not very fond of dogmas. Let's just say, I don't breathe well in them."

"That's not unheard of. My husband was the same way. You shouldn't blame yourself."

"But I do, Cora." Clearly, she knew nothing, nothing about raising children. "And yet still I can't bring myself to go and see him, to make it up with him. And now he says he'll never let me meet my grandson unless I kowtow and make myself the *servant* of his *master*." I suddenly remembered that I needed to sound pitiable, not sarcastic. "This is how my boy speaks to me, you see. It's unbelievable. And now I've lost my entire family to this way of thinking. This is how they all talk. Like zealots. It's unbearable."

"There are worse things."

"I've even lost Agnes to them, Cora."

"Before the divorce?"

"No. After."

"My guess would be that she needed a framework. Something stabilizing, to hang on to. It isn't easy, being alone. You can't always judge—"

"But now they're all down there marching around carrying signs that read 'God Hates Faggots'!"

"Are you sure about that?"

No. No. I still hoped I was wrong. I felt myself wavering in front of her. I wasn't sure. I was afraid to ask. But I had to.

"Are you a believer, Cora?"

It was an appeal. Plainly, simply. I wanted to take it back almost as soon as I had said it. I didn't want to know any more than I did, at that moment, about her. In the next breath she might tell me something, something I didn't want to hear—she might become the lost companion of an afternoon, she might, irrevocably, disappoint me. And then where would I be? For I understood, right then and there, with my feet under her coffee table and hers still pressed tightly together below the knees, her body leaning over the table and yet sealed from me as protectively and prudently as if I were a gust of frigid wind, I understood perfectly that I wanted Cora Lowenstein to be exactly like me. Mistrustful of the world beyond the simplest, hardest evidence. Seeing the universe like a beautiful but indifferent geometry, a cone above us. I wanted her to believe not in selfish, fearful, aggressive human dogmas—I didn't even want her to be, like this spare room, vaguely Buddhist—I just wanted her to be as lost as I was. Finished with faith. Finished with a marriage that maybe had not really been happy, despite all the usual efforts. I wanted her to remember history and that it teaches us nothing if not the panoramic triumph of human failure, interrupted only by small moments, such as these, small communions, when one of us reaches out imperfectly and selfishly toward the other and says, Be with me. I don't need a pew full or a cathedral or a mosque full or a synagogue. I need just you. More than two is dangerous.

"Tristan, the answer is no."

She'd said my name. It made me dizzy. "And—and your husband?"

"He was an assimilationist. A nonpracticing, guilty, stubborn assimilationist. He was torn about Palestine. Why?"

"Were you happy together?"

Again it came out before I could stop myself. Because she had made me brave. She was still stiff, closed, almost shielded. But she was still sitting with me. She hadn't flown away, or even winced.

"I still miss him. Very much. Do you understand? Is that what you wanted to hear? I still visit with him, if you need to know, and I even talk to him. But I still miss him."

"Yes. Sorry. It was none of my business. Of course."

So there it was. On the table. Just as I had been afraid of. As I had anticipated. She had disappointed me. As she was perhaps bound, in a blank, inconsiderate universe, to do. So she was a believer in spirits, in the occult. Speaking and communing with the dead. A woman of light fancies and incoherent ideas. A seeker of signs. A holder of séances. I sat, deflated by her sudden simplicity, so like my ex-wife's, after all, so like my son's, and felt defeated. I could only console myself with the thought that, while I certainly had many dead in my life, at least they didn't visit me, or I them, and the only reason I had to think about them at all had nothing to do with their lingering presence on the planet, or in the Twilight Zone, or on some parallel plane, but because a few rotting pieces of black wood had forced me to.

"In fact," Cora said, parting her knees and standing, "I'm sorry, but I have to hurry you out now. It's getting dark, and I don't like to be late for a visit. It's possible he might know, because— I don't have time to go into all of it right now. I'm sorry. Can I invite you back, some other time?"

I wanted to snap at her *Perhaps a less peopled one, Mrs. Lowenstein?* But then remembered my goal. Perhaps her delusion regarding the sensitivities of the dead might work, at a later date, in my favor. Maybe she even believed furniture housed spirits. So I swallowed my retort and instead spoke as gallantly as I could:

"I hate to think of you going out to a cemetery so late and all alone. You're sure you'll be all right?"

She was standing and facing me. Holding one elegant hand up, ready to usher me out. Her palm froze in mid-gesture. She looked sharply at me, her gaze so steady, her green eyes below her silver sweep of hair so electric I felt as though I'd been caught in a search beam.

"Would you like to come along?"

I realized at once: This was some sort of test. If I failed, I would never get any closer to her. If I hesitated, she would see through all my solicitousness, and know me for what I was. I had no choice.

"I don't know what I'm getting into. But yes. Yes. I would much, much rather come with you."

"Really. Maybe you shouldn't decide so quickly." Her voice was calmer, flatter now. "I'll tell you exactly what you're getting into. My husband has sleep cycles, and wake cycles. They're not pretty. They don't correspond to anything like our own. He's been, for the last twenty-two months, in long-term care out in Connecticut. The doctors insist he's dead, that he has no higher brain functions, and that I should let go, and give him up. My family and friends tell me the same thing, but I don't listen to them. I let most people believe he's dead, because when I tell them the truth they run, as if vegetative states are contagious. Which pointedly suggests that they are. So now." She lifted her chin, politely, but challengingly. "Are you coming?"

"Yes," I swallowed, trapped. "I'm coming."

CHAPTER

13

CORA OWNED A CAR. It had been a long time, many years, since I'd driven one. She unlocked the doors and helped me in on the passenger side, marshaling me as though I were a sickly patient and might hit my head on the roof. It should have been my turn to rebuke her, as she had during our second meeting: *I didn't think I looked old enough for that.* Yet I said nothing as we pulled out of her building's garage and between the bare branches of the hibernating trees. She was at least a good driver. I could only watch, amazed and aghast at what was happening, as she dodged taxis and MTAs and carried us out of the city and into the cement phalanxes of the Bronx. I felt lost. But then clearly I was a man easy enough to mislead.

She told me that during these drives she was apt to become moody and depressed, which she otherwise didn't like or tolerate in herself, and which did no good for anyone, neither herself nor her husband nor the staff at the convalescent home.

"You're doing something uncalled for and unrequired by any law of acquaintanceship I've ever heard of, Tristan. Thank you."

"No, no. No thanks necessary."

She took her eyes briefly from the road and looked at me. It wasn't a smile. It was a glance that was impossible to dismiss, a look clear and honest enough to make the hair on my nape tingle and the nerves in my right leg hum. They say you can't feel pain in two places at once. Ridiculous. I turned to look out the window and tried to organize my wits. She was driving fast. I was getting no time to think. The sky was indistinguishable and starless.

It was so much easier, she went on, to visit Sandor in the evening. His wake cycles seemed to come around most often then—the doctors described them as a meaningless pattern of random responses with no relation to external stimuli—but still, it was nicer to see him when the nurses had him sitting up. The convalescent home was also more quiet and restful then. I nodded, recalling without wishing to my mother propped up in an echoing ward during her last hours. I wondered if it was like that for Cora, too—the dread of visits during the day. Because to visit a dying person in the brightness of noon feels like a taunt. Like carrying a mirror into a cave.

I wasn't at all happy to be in that car, let me make this clear. I had no idea what was happening, or what would be expected of me—or how any of this was going to do me any good. Worse, I fell mute, so that I could hardly have been said to be lively company.

I only hoped I wouldn't have to see him. I didn't know how I could arrange that. Maybe Cora could leave me somewhere, in a lobby or hall or cafeteria. What a coward you are, I snorted at myself. What a sham. I willed the car to slow down; I felt for the handle that would adjust my seat, inching myself backwards by several degrees. *You are afraid to see the man who was once called Sandor Lowenstein. You are afraid to see this Jew reduced to an empty shell.* For Cora was sparing me no detail, in her calm and businesslike way, describing for me how, twenty-eight months before, her husband's heart had stopped in the middle of minor surgery—for gallstones—and how he had been revived only in time to salvage the most basic functions of his being. How he now had to have his teeth brushed for him. And was fed through a tube into his stomach. How at night he was turned several times on an intermittent pressure mattress, to ward off bed-sores, and during the day put into a geriatric wheelchair with a brace to hold his head up, while a nurse's aide came in to exercise his joints. He was given full baths twice a week. His hair was combed for him. He was inspected for skin disorders, signs of pneumonia, blood clots, bladder infections, lice. For the last year she had been visiting regularly, twice a week. She marked anniversaries and birthdays with small gifts.

"He turned fifty-seven in August."

"Oh."

I made further sounds of distress but otherwise could find nothing to say. I looked away. I wanted to be close to her, yes, yes, to be indispensable and trustworthy, but I also wanted to be safely at a remove from all of this, attached, like this mirror, to the side of her car. I looked up and realized we were passing through a piece of country I knew. How long it had been since I'd ventured out of the city. I had been avoiding, of course, the scenes where Agnes and Chris and I had lived and played together, and at times even been happy. There, for example, was the turnoff to the lake where I had once taken them both canoeing, shouting and gripping the bow and paddling ineffectively—for what did I know about deep water, in spite of all my boy-hood years by the dikes and the harbor and the sea? And there, there was the place, it used to be a flea market, where Agnes and I had bought our first piece of furniture for the house, an old rocking chair carved to fit perfectly the curve of one's back, a waiting consolation at the end of a long day. She had nursed our son in that chair. I had lost custody of it in the divorce.

And here was the road that led to the train crossing where she had had her car accident. She'd been angry, that night, because I had accepted an invitation to speak at a conference on her birthday. She'd left the house in her pajamas and was driving to her mother's, trying to beat the train to the crossing, when her wheels got stuck on the rails behind a stalled truck on the other side, which had belonged, improbably, to a repairman named Hero. Hero himself was able to describe to me afterwards how he'd pulled Agnes out just before the train slammed into our station wagon and sent it flying through the air with its green doors flapping like grasshopper wings, until it smashed into a nearby telephone pole and slid down to the earth in a mangled, fluid-leaking heap.

Now, with the energy of a spring compressed inside a box, it all came hurtling back at me. I wondered if Cora noticed the jerk of my shoulders as we passed the train station, as though I were ducking away from it. She didn't seem to. Instead she leaned her silhouetted profile toward me and turned on the radio, scanning the dial until it found an ordered piece of Bach. Thoughtful of her. At least for a while we could simply let the air be plucked and played, without our having to fill it ourselves.

❧

MY MOTHER stepped off a train in Rotterdam in 1928—wearing her only pair of good shoes and carrying a hide bag that looked like a dead animal thrown over her arm. She stood there on the platform and inhaled, remembering forever that first tang of sticky harbor air when it hit her.

So this weight, then, was the sea.

She walked through the station, wide-eyed and interested, until a fat woman stopped her and scolded her for being so obviously a country girl with her hair done up in a nest of braids. This from the German housekeeper from her village who had been written to and was supposed to meet and befriend her. The old woman turned out to be as unsympathetic as a crow. But such minor details didn't bother my mother.

No, because my mother hadn't come for the housekeeper (who shoved her into a trolley on a street crowded with bicycles and carts). She hadn't come, either, for the floors she was soon expected to sweep, or for the greasy windows she was expected to wash, or for the tradesmen she was expected to let into the house of the family she worked for, a family who squinted at her, from the oldest to the toothless youngest, as if she were a dog let into the kitchen. Nor had she come to go to Mass with them on Sunday, and sit in the pew behind them inside a soaring cathedral whose buttresses had reminded her of the bones of a dead horse, or to listen to the priest tell her to be thankful to God ("although of course, I was thankful to Him every day"). No, my mother had come to find the gangly, aloof city boy she had seen on a mountaintop below a fairy-tale castle, and who had given her his name and address, and for whom she had been saving herself.

It took three months before my mother learned and could make her way around the city, another two before she was able to afford a dress and tortoiseshell combs to fix her hair. She knew she was a plain country girl; but she also knew plain women hold up, and that she would still have roses in her cheeks when she was stout and eighty years old and the thin, nitpicking family she worked for were all lying in their coffins with their rib cages sunk. She went to Mass again, this time alone, to thank God for giving her a place, for giving her good cheeks, for the unsympathetic housekeeper who refused to speak German and forced her to improve her Dutch, and for the money in her pocket for car fare. Then she came out and boarded the trolley for the other side of town, as she had done already many times before, to go and spy on him.

Her plan was to wait outside his house, in a park across the street, until he came out alone (as he normally did), and then to step in front of him and surprise him. She had already watched him come out of his door many times. The house was tall, but grimier than the others lined up next to it. The mortar looked pinched between the brick. The curtains were yellowed. She would know what to do about that. She would help his mother bleach the lace. She would iron and fold the tablecloths carefully. She would beat the pillows in the chairs until each was like a fist ready to open. To his father, she would be humble and quiet, bringing him his pipe when he asked for it and a stool for under his tired feet. She would make herself useful. They would love her like a daughter. They would open their arms to her, and be grateful.

She waited until he came out, alone. My father had a way of walking with his shoulders hunched forward so that his head and neck stuck out like a turtle's in front of him, as if his ambition were moving faster than his body could carry it.

She stepped out from her hiding place behind a tree.

"Hello!" she called out clearly.

His head turned toward her, but his body kept walking. His arms and legs seemed to continue past his head. He turned, but his body didn't—so that he seemed to be knotting himself as he looked over his shoulder.

Then he recognized her. And quickly uncoiled his spine.

WHEN IT BECAME CLEAR his family didn't approve they began meeting in secret. They fornicated behind the trees and under the bridges when he should have been with his tutor trying not to fail his Latin classes. They walked afterwards. And talked. They talked about how strange and significant it was that they should have met under a white castle. He talked about his family and how weak and softheaded they'd become. He rounded his shoulders and stuck out his chin, stubbornly. His parents had always treated him like a child. They never let him do anything he wanted to do. He was expected to go to school and study, when what he wanted was to be a speculator, buying and selling and trading things with other people's money. That was the way a man made his mark in the world. Not by sitting in an office chair like his old man, like all the old men who might as well be old women, the way they fussed and worried and kept their balls tied up in purse strings.

No, he said, to be a real success, a man had to be independent. A risk-taker. If he took chances, if he snatched the right opportunity at the right time, then he got what was coming to him. His warehouses would fill and then empty, fill and then empty, and fill up again. And as if to prove it, he pointed across the harbor, where the loaded ships bobbed up and down, endlessly, like horses on a carousel.

And so my mother fell. And bided her time. She kept washing her windows and doing laundry and sweeping out potato peelings and dog hairs. She waited for the day my father's parents would give in, and relent, and see that he loved her, and invite her into their home. But the day didn't come. Then winter set in. It grew cold. Colder. They continued to meet, but now it was uncomfortable; they could only walk. She listened while my father became morose, and then determined, then anxious, then desperate. He was completely honest with her. He told her what his father had said: that he was never going to let a boy of his marry a German servant girl. He told her his family had called her a peasant and a moneygrubber. He wouldn't blame her (he stopped dead in the street and reassured her, anxiously) if she just walked away, and spat on all of them.

But my mother would do nothing of the kind. She still remembered the infested vineyards, a dead calf with a rope around its neck.

People were trying to break him, he said. But he would show everyone. He only had to wait until he was of age, then he would be free to do whatever he felt like. He didn't need any of his family's money, anyway. There wasn't even that much left. No, his father would never have the balls to bankroll a grand plan. *He* would be the first in his family to break out and be a success. He would go it alone. Gladly. Unfortunately (he tugged at his collar and turned his buttons and now told my mother), his father had enlisted him in the foreign civil service. It was the lowest kind of maneuver, but there it was, he really had to go. He would be close to all kinds of business opportunities. This could really be the *best* sort of opportunity. He wouldn't be the first man who, by keeping his mouth shut and his eyes open, came back from a foreign country with a fortune under his belt. She would only have to wait for a little while. He patted her arm, consolingly, and gave her a heavy pewter rosary that had belonged to one of his spinster aunts.

"Be patient." My mother remembered afterwards that his voice had sounded fatherly and resigned. Like the blessing you gave a goose before you wrung its neck.

She watched, from a safe distance, while he boarded the steamer. She watched, hidden from view, as he waved to his family from on deck. She stood until the boat lost itself among all the other ships beating a quick retreat out of the harbor. Then she turned away and the work of resentment began, one foot in front of the other. She didn't plan to lie down. She wouldn't be forgotten. She would reach down and pull him out of the other side of the world, like a gizzard through the gorge of a decapitated chicken. She couldn't imagine the jungle he had gone into, but thought of it as dark, and remote, and unhealthy for both of them.

14

I HELD MYSELF STIFFLY in my seat as Cora swung the car in a wide turn and pulled us into the narrow, deserted visitors' parking lot of the White Oak LifeCare Center.

"Should I leave you at the drop-off, and then go park?"

"No, please. Let's go park."

By this time it was well after eight o'clock. I saw heavy, darkened tree branches cascading toward earth on both sides of us. Something grudging was being parted to let us through. Between the oaks were old-fashioned hooded street lamps also curving down, fixing white pools of light on the asphalt, perhaps trying to convince us we were approaching a tastefully lit gazebo instead of a low-walled, flat-roofed nursing home. I got out of the car and shook my right knee to life before Cora could catch me at it. She came around and locked the doors and together we walked through the black lot slashed with open spaces.

"You don't have to come into the room if you don't want to," she said, keeping her profile very erect. Her breath spiraled in front of her in a dervish. Her hands were shoved deeply inside her coat pockets. I looked down and watched her ankles as they waded through the pools cast by the street lamps.

"Will he be thrown by me?" I asked in a whisper. Empty parking lots at night unnerve me. I felt that night, especially, as if I had wandered onto a target range. "I mean, by a stranger in the room?"

"No. He's out too far. You don't have to worry about upsetting anything. He breathes well on his own. He'll have finished his dinner, by now. They'll have him ready. I only have to warn you about his eyes. They can be hard."

I tried not to think about this. "Do the doctors hold out any hope at all?"

"They don't say a recovery is impossible—but then again, they don't say anything is possible, when obviously they think it isn't. They just tell me to be prepared for this to go on and on." She spoke with her usual composure, only, I thought, with more effort, exhaling into the cold, the ends of her words squeezing like bellows.

"Poor man," I whispered.

She said nothing. As we passed under the awning of the drop-off zone, I wondered if I had sounded automatic, condescending. That wasn't my intention. I was only starting to shiver in the air. The flesh between my ribs ached. Then I wondered, Was it going to snow, later on? Such a bleak night.

Melodramatic. That was how my conscience sounded, even to me. I could have kicked myself. "Poor" was such a poor word to have used. "Poor" suggested: *I have nothing at all to offer you in return for everything that I expect from you.* I hesitated outside the center's entrance, my tongue dangling in my mouth like an empty straw.

"Maybe you don't really want to be here?" She turned to me.

The unfairness of the question goaded me. "No. I *don't* really want to be here. How could anyone *want* to be here? But I said I would come, so I'm coming. That's it. That's all." In my urgency to make this fine speech I forgot to reach out for the entrance and open it for her. Unnecessary. The automatic doors slid apart in their mechanical grooves.

"Tristan." She nodded. "You're good."

Untrue, untrue.

THE WHITE OAK LIFECARE CENTER made few concessions to the holiday season. Its halls and doors were decorated with only a few ersatz wreaths with snow-capped pinecones and snow-white doves stuffed gamely inside them. I was agitated enough, by now, to do what I sometimes do when I have to control myself: become minutely observant.

I've caught others at this form of escape. Students, looking intensely absorbed around a familiar classroom, awaiting the results of their exams. Junior colleagues facing a seminar room, sweating out their tenure reviews. My ex-wife sitting across from me with her brusque, dark-skirted attorney. All of us sending our eyes darting around the room as though the registering of detail might be a way to set a drag on life, to encumber it with anchors, to turn simple doorknobs and hinges and light fixtures and picture frames into metallic claws, holding us back, as if their weight and the sheer weight of our attention to them could exert a pull strong enough to slow the tide of time.

While Cora checked in at reception I absorbed myself in a study of the wreaths with the birds squashed crookedly inside them. Also, bending toward a side table in the waiting room, in the examination of a group of cheerfully clustered velveteen squirrels nestled in among more flora. I considered how difficult it must be to decorate an institution like this one. To ignore the season entirely would be too blunt a commentary on the people still, nominally, living here; to acknowledge it boisterously, unimaginable. So it was a practical compromise, I thought, unclenching my throat, this approach adopted by the administration of the center, to place pinecones thoughtfully indicating the passage of the year, and a squirrel with both paws raised, and holding up a nut, perhaps to call to mind a cautious and prudent and resilient storing away, a kind of metaphor of return, a gesture toward the cyclical, the inevitability of life. . . .

I was becoming lightheaded.

Cora turned and nodded toward me, and now I was forced to straighten and fall in next to and a half-step behind her. She held her head up without glancing to either side, clearly used to her surroundings, unaware of them. We walked through another pair of automatic doors and into the next wing, where she stopped at the station of a floor nurse. The end of this hall was backed by a single floor-length window, black in the night, depthless, like a ship's port below the waterline. I turned away from it. The floor nurse's uniform was a kind of soothing green, not quite medical, suggestive of something halfway between surgery and camouflage. Her face was round, nutlike. She smiled and inclined her head.

"He's up and ready for you, Mrs. Lowenstein."

"Thank you, Padma."

Now Cora faced me so suddenly I was gusted by the perfume on her skin. I'd never noticed her wearing perfume before. When had she put it on? Why? Was it for him?

"You're sure about this." Her forehead had wrinkled into deep lines.

But those are out of concern for me.

"Please," I insisted. "This was already decided."

"I'm just double-checking."

"No need."

"There is always need," she said.

She pushed the door in, quietly; it was as if she didn't want to startle anyone who might be up and hiding mischievously behind it. I grew tense immediately. Yet this room looked no different, was no more strange than the rooms in which I'd healed after my surgeries. The curtains at the window were blue, and drawn shut, appropriately, because it was night. A vase had been filled with artificial flowers and put on a table on one side of the bed. On the other side clustered family photographs, an open jar of Vaseline, a small radio, and a hairbrush and comb. I became aware of the outline of a man, sitting in a wheelchair beside the window. But he wasn't the strongest presence in that room. No. Not even remotely. It was those flowers. The artificial chrysanthemums. They were out of season, out of place. With gold petals that hooked fiercely in around their invisible centers.

"San. I've brought someone in with me today." I watched her kiss her husband's forehead calmly, then sit down in a chair in front of him. She held something limp between her hands. His hand. I slid sideways over, paying minute attention to my feet, sitting down behind her without glancing up.

"This is Dr. Martens. Dr. Tristan Martens. *Not* a medical doctor, thank goodness. I thought you might like to see a new face." She paused, her eyes squinting. "Someone different."

At this point I had no choice but to acknowledge Sandor Lowenstein. I looked up. I could hardly bear what I saw. Here was a man reduced to his most blockish parts. An engine without a vehicle.

The bones of his knuckles glinted like bearings under that fluorescent light. His sparse hair looked brittle. When I could bring myself, at last, to gaze into his face, I saw only a vague resemblance, only the suspended ruin of a man whose photograph I had seen for the first time only a few hours before, leaning against his car at the beach, captured in sunburned midlife.

The room was quickly too warm. My nose itched with the smell of something acrid. If I could have, I would have made any excuse to go. But I didn't dare move. I had to prove to Cora I was more faithful, more lasting than the others she had brought here before me. That I could be valiant. So I waited for some cue.

She bent to rearrange the blanket that covered his wasted knees. The sight filled me with embarrassment. Should I speak? Was I a witness only, here? A bystander? An enemy? A fellow ghost? *What*, I wanted to beg her, *can I be, in this room?*

The vein at her left temple had sprung out. She turned to me. "Sometimes we talk a great deal, San and I. Don't we, San? And sometimes, we don't." I saw the sagging weight in her cheeks, under her chin. Or maybe it was only that horrendous light. "Sense stimulation is good for him." She stroked his fingers. His gaze, unseeing, bobbed and went over her head. It reminded me of the blankness of a buoy facing the shore.

"I'm so sorry, Cora."

"Don't be. The fault's all mine."

"That can't be true."

"You don't know anything about it. He wanted to go to a different hospital. I insisted he go to mine, where I'd had my appendix out.

Because I liked the *rooms* there. Can you imagine that? A simple choice. Do you know what disaster looks like? It's a tired, over-worked twenty-eight-year-old anesthesiologist. And another man is wiped out. Erased, maybe completely. Maybe forever."

I stared down at their twined hands, his so passive and desiccated, hers so lithe. Trying not to be envious. "You can still tell people who Sandor is."

She looked to him, as if listening; then turned away. "Well. That's our problem, you see. That's what I've discovered. We have this habit of thinking we can speak for someone close to us. We even do it. All the time. We think we know their thoughts before they think them. And who knows? Maybe we do. But how can we be sure? Maybe all along those were only our thoughts, reflected back to us. Maybe the people we love simply humor us, and agree with us, be-cause they have to. Because *we* humor *them*. And now, when San can't fight back, or laugh, or complain, or raise his eyebrows, or change his mind, or leave a door unlocked, or joke with me, or play his music, you want me to tell you who he is?"

"No." I dropped my eyes to my ankles. Even under my socks they looked strangely alive. Like barnacles.

"No. You can't necessarily trust what people tell you. Or believe you know them from what they say, know what happens inside them. Even people you feel the most drawn to." She shifted in her chair, but it was only to slide the fold of her coat out from underneath her. "Look. I take his hands, each time, but I still can't feel my way into what he's going through. I can speak about him, but not for him. I'm not a ventriloquist. A man should be allowed to speak for himself. Or at least be allowed to try. I won't tell you what he can't tell you him-self. I can't betray him that way. He deserves that much—privacy."

"Then maybe I shouldn't be here at all?" I glanced hopefully at the door. "Maybe he wouldn't like me to see him like this. *I* wouldn't." This was as truthful as I could be.

But she didn't hear me. She had turned one of his palms over and was staring into it. "I'll say only this much for you, San. What I know. It was something he could never comprehend, Tristan. The idea that if you study a human being enough, you can necessarily *imagine* him. Understand anything beyond the obvious. I remember once, years ago, a researcher—oh, maybe it was someone from your university, it might have been, I don't remember—this young woman, she kept calling and calling and calling, and San wouldn't answer her calls, and then finally she came one day to the door and wanted to interview him because he was the son of a family who had fled Hitler in time. She wanted to understand the guilt experiences of the people who had gotten out. The quick ones. The survivors, she said. Particularly the creative ones, the educated ones. The smart ones. And San, he slammed the door in her face. He told her that the outlines of murder are enough, and the details were for voyeurs. He said, 'You have studied us enough. To death. To distinction. Like mutants. There is nothing *abnormal* about us. You don't need to look in our mouths, you've already seen our teeth, our glasses, our hair, our bodies piled up in those stacks. Go, try studying the teeth of the man who took the children away and handed them over to the doctors for the brain experiments.' He rarely lost his temper, that way. But I remember he shouted at her through the door, 'See where that takes you!' When he rarely shouted at all. He was miserable afterwards. He sat in a mood for hours, at his piano. Now what does that tell you?"

"I don't know," I said. I felt sickened. I was the one who had let myself in for this—this travesty. This ugly deception. I could have said no. But now, now it was too late. I felt a tightening at the back of my throat, half choking, half defensive. My mouth tasted of copper. "But if we say we can't understand anyone or anything, then—then all progress stops. We don't have to know everything to know a small part of it."

"That's the academic in you. I forgot to tell you, San. This man is a scientist."

"An entomologist." I spoke directly to him. I owed him that much. I could see the beat at his carotid artery, where the brace suspended his neck like a flue above his body. And recalled, suddenly, that vulnerable stage when a creature is struggling to molt. To begin life new.

"I'm trying to be a friend here, Mr. Lowenstein."

"I met Professor Martens in the shop, San. He seems to have good taste. He bought one of the Normandy chairs. He's kind, and oddly generous, and sometimes I half believe I can trust him."

"Excuse me, please." I stood. "I think I ought to leave you two alone, now."

"I didn't mean to be rude. Will you forgive me?"

My heart leapt. But she wasn't speaking to me. She was looking at him, leaning forward as if she had done something, could somehow do something, to irritate him; squinting toward him, narrowly, because the incident was somehow between the two of them, alone; and because she must have known she was deserving of some forgiveness after all her attentiveness and loyalty to him. And maybe because even in that overheated, stagnant room there was something left of a marriage—I could see it, I wasn't so far gone that I couldn't remember and recognize it—that forbearance that is so crucial to love, the first leg it stands on, while the other is a dependency close to fear.

And love was like that, I thought, wearily, turning away—love like two people in a three-legged race, tied together, limping, hopping, walking forward, trotting, jogging, sometimes running, sometimes stumbling, until the goal was reached, or one leg or the other collapsed.

"I'll go back and wait in the lobby."

"All right. I'll only be a few minutes."

I closed the door on my way out.

CHAPTER

15

"HAVE YOU BEEN COMFORTABLE?" She stood in front of me an hour later.

I looked up from the journal I had pilfered from the nurse's station. From the *Annals of the New York Academy of Sciences:* Persistent Vegetative or Non-Cognitive State: Destruction of critical elements of the central nervous system, leaving the patient in an irreversible condition in which there is no evidence of awareness. Higher functions of the brain are absent, and there is no purposive response to external stimuli. No awareness, though patient may be aroused. Arousability, viz: reflexes in response to noxious stimuli. Eye-opening. Responses to needles applied to feet. Sneezes. Arousability does not necessarily imply cognitive function or awareness. *Patient is not a sentient individual.*

The cafeteria was silent. I scanned the room; we were the only people left inside the hub of tables. "You didn't rush, because of me?"

"No. It was terrible for you. Wasn't it?"

"I hated it."

"I'm sorry."

"It deserves to be hated, Cora."

"I know."

"How do you do it?" I pulled out a chair for her.

She sat down, heavily. "I don't ask questions. I don't hear answers. Holidays are nightmares."

"You'll be here."

"We'll light the candles. One or two of my brothers or sisters will come with me. Then I'll go back home with them."

"He looks as if he's holding up." *God Almighty.* What a ridiculous thing to have said, as though speaking of the tread on a tire.

She folded her hands, kneading them into a taut basket. How I wanted, so badly, to touch her. I had to hold myself perfectly, excruciatingly still, just to keep from doing so. There are many things more terrible than what I was going through, at that moment. I know this. But what I was experiencing—fruitlessly, desperately—was the glimpse of an impossible future, mine, yes, mine, coupled improbably with Cora's, and then coupled with a shame so deep it reached back, back into my blood, as if my heart were sucking rather than pumping, going in reverse until I saw my father, until I was again under my mother's table, hiding, breathless, awed by the black stripe of his leg.

"I would like to say," she sighed, "that you were better than most people. Better than my own family. You were a real *mensch* in there."

"No."

"And I'm going to tell you something, Tristan. Every day I come here, I despise myself."

"No, Cora, no."

"Because I want to stop. But I don't want to stop. I want something to happen—but I don't want to be the one to make it happen."

I sensed rather than saw the cafeteria ceiling mushrooming over us. And Cora and I sitting alone beneath its canopy, dark, moist, minuscule things. Insignificant.

"They're telling me to give up. They're telling me to pull the stomach tube, to stop feeding him."

"That's horrible."

"It is. At least in your country they let people die with dignity."

"But it's not that easy. Nothing is ever so simple, Cora." I almost shrank from her. "You could—you could do it?"

"Could you? Could you pull the earth out from under someone you loved? If you thought it was the best thing?"

"I don't know."

"Then you're a coward. Like me."

"But Sandor—? He would trust you. He would trust you to think for the both of you."

"That still doesn't make the answer clear, does it." She ran her fingers through her hair, leaving them tangled at the nape of her neck. "Do you ever feel like you want to be a child again, Tristan, and stop feeling all the weight? But you can't. You can't." I watched her fingers at her scalp. I knew then that Cora Lowenstein could pull her roots out without flinching.

"Even children feel responsibility," I said.

"I'm just tired. I'm not making sense."

"I think you are. But Cora, one thing I don't understand. How do you have—enough to keep going? To keep all this up?"

"The settlement covers everything."

"Then maybe you should just leave it at that."

"How convenient. How—bureaucratic."

"Because otherwise you live in limbo. Like San. Is that what he would have wanted?"

She dropped her hands and stared narrowly at me. Reclassifying me now with all the others. I could see it. Lumping me with her family, and the doctors, and the friends she no longer considered her friends. Handing me over to them. But I would not be so handled. I would *not*. Of course, of course I wouldn't let one human being die—not if the chance were given me. This was a point so absolute inside me that I shivered, it felt like the dropping of an icicle from a window ledge down into snow, uncontrollable, cold into cold, accidental, natural, gravitational, numb perhaps; but clear, and powerful. I would save him, if I could, even though I wanted what was his. I would save him until the last, automatic, incomprehensible breath.

There are human beings perhaps, who do not want to be saved. But there is no human being, I want to believe, who doesn't want someone to want to save him.

"I wouldn't do it, Cora."

She looked away as if she hadn't heard me. Or as if what I had said couldn't matter. An orderly walked through the passage, buttoning his white jacket. He straightened his collar. It was late. His day had just begun.

"I WANT TO TELL YOU SOMETHING," she said in her usual, even voice during the drive back. It was intensely dark and our headlights beat against the first snow flurries, breaking them into whirling white swarms. "You put yourself out for me, tonight. You have been acting remarkably like—like a friend."

"I want to be." I needed to say this. But then nothing more.

"Then I should return your kindness. I feel it." We both waited through her silence. "I think—I think you might need a little bit of talking to, Tristan. I'm trying to act decently, now. Like a friend. Look at what can happen. You turn around, and everything you counted on, even the painful things, the oldest problems, they're gone. No more time for arguments. For any more words."

"I don't think I can take any more talk tonight, Cora. I'm exhausted."

"I think you should try talking to your son."

She drove without speaking again for several minutes, through the darkness gliding past us, tapping the knuckle of her thumb against the steering wheel. A new gesture. I tried to memorize it.

"You're going to tell me it's none of my business."

"I wouldn't say so."

"All right then. Just relax, and I'll get you back."

I discovered then that a man can be so overwhelmed, he doesn't mind being dumb. I settled into my seat and spent the rest of the way concentrating on the simple struggle to keep my eyes open and my mouth closed in front of her.

1 6

FOR ONCE I didn't want to be alone on Christmas Eve. I was depressed at the thought of Cora, pulled away after our brief, tentative
good-bye outside my building, withdrawn by now—I couldn't picture it—behind the closed gates of her family. I didn't know what to
do with myself. I wasn't in the frame of mind to be a detached observer of the holidays, the way I normally could have been. Staring
down at the city as if it held no gift I wanted it to make me. Not
this year.

Everything was different.

I had to cough on my hands to warm them. I kept my back to the
window (I could still feel the cold seeping through the metal around
the panes, crawling along my lower spine) and stared at the printed
reams of paper I had generated at my desk in the lean hours of the
morning. The photographs. Westerbork. Auschwitz. Dachau.

I had to steel myself. To keep my eye on what mattered. On what
was now at stake. I couldn't afford to lose my old capacity to be rig-
orous, to concentrate—not now, not when I needed it the most. The

final toll of the year was coming, and I still hadn't redeemed any part of what was mine. Had I even accomplished anything? Having lunch with Cora Lowenstein? Visiting her husband in his stale room? As if that could be measured, at all, as progress.

The jumble of printed pages on the floor and on the dining table looked too much like a circus of wrapping paper. Agnes used to make this kind of mess, getting presents ready for under one of the trees she so painstakingly chose and then decorated, wincing when I failed to notice her angels made out of lace, the previous year's Christmas cards cut and formed into buckyball ornaments edged with silver icing.

On the stairs, lately, or in the elevator, certain of my neighbors had shot pained and harassed glances at me that said, "If I drop this package and you pick it up, please don't talk to me when you hand it back." But others, when I passed them, broke into beatific smiles. Like saints.

The hallways had gotten colder. The smells of cooking grease outside my door were, at least, less powerful.

I STAYED HUNKERED INSIDE all morning, keeping quiet and warm. Now and again, sorting through the notes I'd begun to make, I glanced up at the antique chair. It seemed to flounce its carved shoulders at me. Open-armed. Round-bottomed. Inviting. Suing to be rested in. I turned away from it. Resisting. I meant to stand by my original idea that it wasn't going to be lounged in. I couldn't deny, however, that having an empty, out-of-place chair always hanging around the apartment was beginning to make me feel jumpy. Always this sense of reserved space now in the corner.

Another symptom, I rapped myself on the forehead, of senility's encroaching inability to stay on track. What an old man had to do now was simply sit down again (in something *other* than that chair) and think clearly about what was happening, what must happen, if he was going to get his hands on what he wanted and take it and break it and remove it permanently from circulation. I went back to my desk. I would not lose my way. I would not let myself be confused and distracted, or give in to the edginess and moodiness of the season.

And then, as luck would have it, my phone rang.

⮌

"WHAT ARE YOU DOING?" Elida demanded.

My first thought was that the poor girl must be jumpy herself, if she had gone so far as to pick up a telephone. Elida Hernandez, when she wasn't beating on my door, generally favored dumping her questions and obsessions and doubts and revisions into my e-mail (*Re: Subfamily Parandrinae*). That she had reached for something as primitive as a receiver could only be the prelude to an announcement of some sort of thesis-searing panic.

"I'm working."

"I thought I asked you to get a more active life. To get out more. And you're working on Christmas Eve?"

"It's all right. It's unholy work."

"Then it's a good thing I called. Martens. I'm worried."

"What's wrong now?" I readied myself for a small crisis.

"I'm on to something. But I'm having trouble distinguishing between two of my mimics."

"So you're working on Christmas Eve, too."

"No, I'm losing my mind."

"Since when?"

"Since right away, since this minute, since I bothered to look closely enough. The genitalia. I've been dissecting carefully, and the differences are confusing. I was convinced I had variations in male and female of the same species—but now I'm not so sure, I may have male and female of two *separate* cerambycid species, slightly distinct, or maybe uncannily alike, and they might not even be the same genus at all, unless I'm mistaken, or—or—"

"Welcome to the chicanery of the natural world, Elida."

"You need to take a look at this."

"Fine."

"Right *now.*"

"Be serious."

"I am. I won't be able to sleep tonight." She sounded even more tense and self-chastising than usual.

"I can't get to the lab," she fretted. "And I can't leave the house on Christmas Eve. I mean, it's Christmas *Eve.* My family's here. What are you doing?"

"I told you. I'm working."

"By yourself? You're doing Christmas by yourself? I knew it."

"It's so peaceful."

"It must be dull. Tell me you're bored."

"Let me understand. You're expecting me to come to Brooklyn and take a closer look at some of your specimens. On Christmas Eve?"

"Well, it's not as if it's Christmas. Hold on."

I heard a sound like cloth covering the mouthpiece. The murmur of bargaining voices filtering through.

"Yes, that's right," she came back. "We're cooking *mole,* and my mother will kill me if I leave the house. So you have to come here. I told her you're flying solo tonight and she said to come to our place and have dinner with us."

I sensed, suspicious, the whiffling wings of a trick beetle. Elida in her misguided attentiveness trying to lure me out of my nest. She hurried on without a breath now, directing me, filling me in, as if I'd always been in the habit of celebrating major feast days with her and her family. When, in point of fact, I'd never been with her anywhere other than at this desk, or in a classroom, or in my office, or in the library, or at the lab, or at the museum—so that I was hardly able to picture her mired in Brooklyn.

"You should be calling Blathert about this."

"Blathert is in Kenya."

"I couldn't possibly intrude on your family today."

"You have to. Or I wouldn't be calling you like this. It's urgent. And my mother wants to thank you for all you've done for me. She's saying so. She's saying so right now." I could hear shouting in Spanish in the background.

"Tell her I haven't done anything to deserve this."

"If you turn her down, she'll be offended. She's very Mexican that way."

"I don't know what to say."

"Say come at five. Take a cab. Or are you good on the trains?"

"Should I bring something?"

"Wine. We need cheap wine. At five, all right?"

"All right."

"Martens. *Don't* back out on me."

"Of course not."

I found that my pulse was racing wildly. But then congratulated myself on not having sounded overeager. Or overly accommodating. I had taken matters rather smoothly, I thought. Even with a certain modesty . . .

But then—I noticed the empty chair—then again, it may have been that, in spite of my best efforts, all my banter and my reserve, and my pretense at reluctance, I had still ended up appearing a lamentable, lonely character to Elida Hernandez.

THAT THOUGHT SKEWERED ME for a moment. I slumped. It was essential, if one was going to do the thing at all, that one not appear too much like a hapless, worrisome emeritus with no place else to go. Because Elida Hernandez was after all one of the few young persons, perhaps the only young person left who at that moment believed me capable of sorting out incommensurable signs. Or at least of rectifying basic errors. If nothing else, I owed it to her to seem competent. To be commanding. Authoritative.

Well then. I would be. I would be a teacher again. A shedder of light.

This called for preparations.

I stood in front of the closet mirror. Distracted for a moment by the scar traveling in its track down my sternum. The line flushes and turns a deeper red and welters whenever I most want it to disappear. But now I could occupy myself in thinking about what I should wear to cover my upper extremities (sweater? jacket? tie?). Also, there was the problem of whom I would be required to meet and talk to (parents? siblings? neighbors?), and the matter of the wine (fowl? meat? fish? a Merlot?). I knotted and unknotted myself, back and forth, back and forth, until the only reasonable course seemed to be to go with the tie and the Merlot and the sweater and the jacket, all at once.

By the time I made it down to the street I was in the midst of the last blizzardlike rush before the shops closed. The air was electric and frosty and dry, like the inside of a meat truck. My ears cleared. I strode, warm and itchy under my hat. The blur of people on foot and in taxis, the cashier at the liquor store with red and green sparkles dressing up her eyelids, the slush of cleared snow ranked along the curbs, like the blackened gums of a beached whale—it was all very alive and enfolding. I felt swallowed up. Only my place on the train irked me (no wonder I normally stayed home on such occasions), crammed as I was up against a sour-smelling man in a wrinkled business suit and a woman viciously gnawing the calloused skin from her thumb. A cellist, maybe. Or stenographer. I clung to the rail above me, and protected my bottle of wine against the saddle of my chest. Hoping I wasn't overheating it.

Someone's elbow jabbed into my spine. Next my shoes were being trampled on and scuffed. I squeezed farther into the box of the car. I sweated. I huffed. I'm not normally claustrophobic. But this was too compact. Too close for comfort. It was intolerable. I wanted out. I began to realize what I would soon be in the middle of. What was I going to do, what was I doing now among all these *folk*, anyhow? What did any of it have to do with me? The air was impossible to breathe. Panhandlers were singing at the end of the car, commuters were drowsing, and coughing, and arguing, wrapped parcels and cardboard tubes were sticking up over our heads like severed limbs, toward the ads on the ceiling. *Give the gift that shows you see the light in her eyes!* And somewhere, somewhere behind other, frantic national festivals like this one, I thought, land mines are being laid, and new ways for humans to lump and destroy one another being devised.

Not at all the right attitude to be taking to a party.

The ravaged finger of the woman beside me was so close I could see the raw endoderm clinging as she tugged at it. This was all too near. Too human. Well, what then? You could have stayed at home. Maybe this wasn't such a fine idea after all. You will be out of place, in Brooklyn, with that group. You'll be a third wheel. Worse. A free-loader. But then, you didn't want to stay at home. Remember? You didn't want to be alone. With Cora off, gone out to her family. She had said she would call only after she got back. And Elida, acting beside herself with frustration—she claimed that she needed help. So where did that leave you now, what was there to do, except to hold breath, and bottle, and wallet, and change lines?

A relief it was to get into the next slightly less impossibly crowded car, to squeeze in and sit down, and then, finally, to reach the station Elida had said was nearest her house. And then finally, finally to come up into the dripping, tar-scented air of Brooklyn. I found her duplex easily on the next block, and the window of her floor, the second one, as she'd told me, by its pattern of twinkling lights hung in the shape of a makeshift star.

A SMALL BOY with a face like brown bread opened the door to me.

"Hello." I stiffened.

He ran away. Sneakers pumping thickly against the floor. Elida flipped her long black skirt to one side to let him pass. In that yellow light, and with her braid lying across her shoulder, she looked so sleek and warm and young I felt acutely we didn't inhabit the same era. She was bird to my dinosaur.

I offered my hand and she took it in something between a jerk and a shake.

"My nephew, Alberto. You'll have to excuse him. So! You made it." She pulled me in.

"Yes. This is for you."

"It's just a family dinner, you know."

"I thought the occasion called for something special."

"Well, thank you. Thank you for coming. This is so crucial to me."

"No, no." I shook my head. "You're overreacting, Elida. Clearly I'm horning in."

"You're not. Think of it as a kind of field trip. Come on in and I'll make you comfortable. Don't be shy."

"All right."

She took me by the arm. An odd sensation. I could feel her small hand under my elbow like a narrow keel. We had entered uncharted territory. I was being led through a high-ceilinged hallway lined with bull's-eyed doors on both sides. Behind one of these I could hear the bleeps and shots and squeals of children playing at an electronic game. Elida glided past, explaining.

"I'm taking you to meet my mother and brothers and sisters first."

"How many?" I asked alarmed.

"Four. Two of each. Eight, counting their wives and husbands. You won't be able to keep all the names straight. Don't even try. Are you hungry?"

I will be the donkey at a horse show. "Yes. What a delicious smell. The *mole?*" I tried fixing my attention on the current of pepper and cinnamon and chocolate ahead of us, now growing stronger.

"My mother makes it the best. The kitchen and living room are at the front. Wait, you'll have to duck here—excuse the detritus." She held up a piece of garland decking the hallway. "The grandkids did all the decorating. Incredibly unartistic. *Mama!*" she called out. *"Mi profesor está aquí."*

"Bueno. Ya vengo."

A short, blunt woman suddenly appeared from a doorway on my left. Her long earlobes were so pronounced, like swallowtails, she seemed for a moment to hang suspended between them. She stood with a dishtowel twisted like a boxer's glove around one of her hands. And held out the other.

"I am Rocío Hernandez. It's a pleasure to meet you, sir. We've heard so much about you."

"Mucho gusto." I nodded. "It's kind of you to have me."

"Elida, use your head. Take the man's things."

Elida handed my damp bottle to the young woman standing suddenly next to her. We were held up now at the opening to another, larger room, this one filled with the blue light from a television, and the twinkling of a multicolored Christmas tree, and also with people, so many, young and old and tall and short and fat and thin, all stretching and yawning and standing up, obligingly, for me.

"Everyone, this is my mentor." Elida helped me out of my coat. "Don't embarrass me, you hear?" I flinched. But she was addressing her relatives. "Behave yourself or I'll kill you. Say Merry Christmas, Rebecca."

"Merry Christmas." The young woman holding my wine smiled. She looked strikingly like Elida. The same heart-shaped face. Only more maternal.

"Merry Christmas," said the man who was her husband.

"Merry Christmas."

"Feliz Navidad."

"Feliz Navidad."

"Merry Christmas."

And so it went, around the room, until everyone had said something formal and precise and welcoming to me. I blushed. It was all a bit overwhelming.

"Please go in and sit down." Elida's mother gestured with her boxer's fist.

"Thank you very much for having me. Again."

"Would you like something warm? Some coffee?"

"No, thank you. I'll just—"

"Sit down here." A woman of about my own age pulled me down with her onto one of the high-backed sofas. Then, without warning, turned her shoulder on me.

"*Who is this man again?*" she asked in Spanish. She wore a black cap I thought I recognized as one of Elida's.

"This is my bug professor, Abuelita."

"I don't believe it." Abuelita leaned in and spoke to me familiarly. "I thought she was telling us lies, you know. All the time, I thought, she is taking classes to become an exterminator."

"Understandable." I nodded.

"An exterminator in the family would have been useful."

"Behave." Elida slapped her lightly. "Mama! Tell this one."

"I can't. She's a grown woman."

"Not if you count her teeth," a boy cracked and bolted from the room.

"Shouldn't we open the wine?" I offered. Everyone else except Elida's mother was now sitting down on the couches and chairs again and staring at me. If ever a moment called for something bracing . . .

Elida stood. "I'll go get the corkscrew."

"I'll help—"

"No, no. Just relax and stay here."

So she had left me, had she—deliberately?—to face her family. And just what was it she expected me to do for her, with them? I had no idea what sort of holiday rituals to initiate, no real experience in such an arena. Agnes and Christopher and I had eventually fallen into the habit of getting things out of the way quickly before and after

Christmas dinner. While the holidays of my childhood, well, they hardly bore thinking about.

I edged forward on the sofa and scraped the inside of my forehead searching for an appropriate phrase. Already I could see how I looked in their eyes: like some gray, overtaut balloon that had bumbled accidentally into their ken. I squeezed my hands together. I must have looked as though I would pop.

Yet they were all very kind to me. Once they saw Abuelita was going to keep me occupied, degree by degree they inched their gazes away (I could hardly blame them) and went back to watching television and arguing among themselves, so that while I was being informed (by Abuelita) of the number of trees recently lost to bugs in the neighborhood, I could look around and study my surroundings—the small religious pictures off-center high on the walls—the fierce-looking stereo system with its lights glowing—the blinking tree dividing itself into unequal parts in the corner.

"Time for a toast." Elida was back and handing out small plastic glasses to the adults. "To peace on earth, goodwill toward everything."

"*Feliz Navidad!*"

"Hear, hear!" I said too loudly.

"Bah. This is too weak," Abuelita complained as we drank. Then: "When are we eating?"

"When Mama says so." To me, Elida whispered, "And now, I'm going to rescue you."

"But I'm having a lovely time."

"But that's not why you're here. Let's retreat."

I followed her back down the hallway.

"Does *everyone* live here at home?" I asked meekly.

"Are you serious? I'm the only one left. All my sisters and brothers have kids. They think I'm a sad case. An apostate."

"Because of your work."

"Well—partly. They think a man would be crazy to trust me to clean a house filled with beetles. Hang on, I've locked the door to keep the kids out. I have to warn you, it's a disaster in here. Hardly a recommendation to the committee. Never reveal what you see."

"My lips are sealed."

"Watch out then."

But when she switched on the light all I saw ahead of me was a small room stuffed from floor to ceiling with beautifully mounted *Buprestidae* and *Scarabaeidae*. The jewel beetles, in particular, shone fragile inside their boxes like portraits of friends with whom I hadn't corresponded in a long time. *Plusiotis gloriosa*. I recognized a fantastic weevil from New Guinea, *Eupholus bennetti*. This looks like nothing so much as a Medicean tapestry with six legs.

"From Maxilla and Mandible?"

"Yes."

"Very nice." I stepped in to get a closer look and nearly stumbled. Her floor was covered with discarded notes and crumpled manuscript. Balanced against the baseboards were uneven piles of books and journals, stacks of unkempt color photocopies, rows of empty killing jars. A large bookcase careened over us with an overflow of catalogs, disks, books, instruments, note cards, and folders. Only one corner of her desk was cleared for a dissecting microscope and her computer. A pair of light-action forceps rested on the edge of this, as though she had been trying to pull a mote of definitiveness from between the keys. A narrow bed was squeezed in next to the desk like an afterthought.

Elida didn't score points for interior design. Yet now I could be perfectly at ease. This could have been my own room. I felt also a faint yearning, fading but unmistakable, for the field.

"And this?" I pointed to one of her cerambycids.

"*Ulochaetes leoninus.*"

"Show me the new specimens."

"Over here, next to the scope." She shoved aside a pile of old journals. "They're similar to most of the known wasp mimics, but as I told you, the disguise is in some ways more complete, keyed to the dry environment and the competition for hollowed wood. Here."

I took the magnifying glass from her.

"Haven't you considered the example of the velvet ant? The males and females are so different they haven't all been matched together."

"But I'm not sure that's what's happening here. What do you think?"

"These are male and female of the same species." I straightened decisively.

"What makes you say so?"

"The optimist in me."

"Martens. Please. I've been floundering here. I need to be certain."

"All right. You wouldn't be likely to find separate species with such a slight variation in structure within such narrow environmental parameters. You know that."

"I know. But look also at the prothorax. These just don't seem to be *simpático.*"

"Interesting choice of word."

"You've said it a thousand times. Slight *matters*. Slight alters. Evolution is built on hairsplitting."

"But it's also unpredictable, Elida." I straightened again. "Larger than we are. Improvements and adjustments come. They come. But you don't always catch them in the act."

"Sometimes we might."

"These are from Arizona?"

"Near Sedona. Kellman from Flagstaff was with me when I collected them."

"Well, then, you'll simply have to collect more if you want to make a more complex argument. What chance of that?"

"I don't know. These didn't exactly swarm out of the sky. Human population down there is exploding. All you senior citizens," she lobbed accusingly.

I ignored this. "Then you'd better get going."

"I don't have any travel funds left. I've gone through the fellowship. I didn't plan ahead for this. I may have to stop for a while and concentrate on applying for some—"

"No, don't, I'll loan you the money."

I was still peering down at my mazed thumb through the magnifying glass. I wasn't even sure I had heard myself say this. Or why I had said it. Or where such an idea—no, more to the point, more distressingly, from where in my accounts I had pulled such a sum.

"Oh." She jumped away. As though I had *bitten* her, for God's sake. "That's impossible, Martens. I couldn't."

"Don't be prissy," I said haughtily. "If you're driven to find out, then you'll have to do more work."

"Sometimes I don't see how I'll ever make it."

"You will, or you won't. That's the whole idea. That's the test."

"I'll be old before I can defend myself."

"Elida. The good fortune of being twenty-six is that you don't taste the pith of your own exaggerations. I think you can still make the defense in spring. The committee will be impressed with your new work."

"You're sure they will be?"

"Of course."

"You know, Martens. It's all I want for Christmas." She collapsed onto her bed, the moody girl I knew, and knew would now be self-flagellating, self-doubting.

"Buck up." I tried to lighten things. "You'll have Christmas in April."

"I feel so obscure." She tugged at her skirt. It had fanned around her in a deep black corona. "As if taxonomy really matters to anyone but taxonomists. You're right, though. I exaggerate. It must be an occupational hazard. Anyway. What do *you* want, Martens? I mean, from the old bearded man." She wiped her chin and smiled at me now with one of her random flares of sympathy across the space between us.

"The usual. How much is that doggy in the window."

"I can't imagine you with a pet."

"I've never had one. It is one of the great tragedies of my life."

"Decent life then."

"I'd have to agree."

"Do you consider"—she pointed her wide nose toward one of her glass cases—"these fellows company?"

No. I wouldn't have put it that way myself.

MRS. HERNANDEZ CONFIDED TO ME, laying a napkin on my lap, "Elida tries very hard to explain it all to us."

I wished, as I fidgeted nervously and rearranged my silverware, that someone would do me the same service. I was trying to understand what it was I was going to be doing, now, with this group of people for the rest of the evening. The adults among us were sitting squeezed around an oblong dining table. The children were in the living room, kicking one another under folding television trays. Carols were throbbing on the bass of the stereo, and then suddenly the entire family, as if on cue, bowed their collective heads, and prayers were being said. I felt as out of place as if they had made room for me in that crowded stable.

"Have some." Elida spoke from my right. "Authentic, about a hundred different spices. I hope you like it."

"Thank you."

"*Mira.*" Mrs. Hernandez, sitting at the head of the table, leaned into me and went on. "Isn't this much nicer than playing with dead bugs? I tell her that in Mexico some people *eat* what she studies."

"If it's so natural, you'd think my mother wouldn't be disgusted by it."

"But *chica*"—she shivered in protest—"we don't hang what we eat on the walls."

"Some people do." Elida was filling her own plate with chicken and rice. "And some wear what they eat. Mexican jewelry incorporates beetles. Even living ones. You know that."

"I try not to think about it." Mrs. Hernandez grimaced at me. She set her fork down and pressed her hands together. "So. Maybe you can explain to me why some people follow this profession?"

Elida, her fork suspended in midair, looked at me.

"Perhaps it's because beetles are so . . . clean," I offered.

"You must be crazy." Abuelita shot this across the table. "With all that—ugh—inside?"

"Tell her to stop, Mama." Elida traced an outline on the tablecloth with her knife. "Anyway. It's not so 'ugh.' Beetles are different than we are. They don't have closed veins. The heart pumps blood directly from the thorax into the body cavity. Dumps it right in. It's gooey, and it's primitive, but it's also neat and it simplifies everything."

"I still don't see it, *mi hija*."

"There are other aspects, too," I amended professionally. "When I first came here, I worked in a slaughterhouse, and I witnessed first-hand—"

"You say when you first came here?"

"Yes, Mrs. Hernandez, I—"

"Rocío. From where?"

"From Europe. Holland."

"When did you come?"

"In the early fifties."

"With your family of course."

"No. Alone."

Elida raised her eyebrows and made a slow show of tearing at the bones of her chicken.

"It must have been hard," her mother said sympathetically, her swallowtail ears sweeping closer to mine. "Did you have a sponsor? One of my husband's relatives sponsored us, otherwise we would never have made it here. This country doesn't like too many Latinos."

Nor is it particularly welcoming, I might have added, to the children of minor war criminals. Although there were always people ready to forgive the very young.

"A Dutch-American group sponsored me, Mrs. Hernandez. But that's not what I was getting at. What I meant to say is, the only kind of work they could get me was as an apprentice butcher, and such work exposes one to—to a certain environment. And in—well—as to cleanliness, it was in the slaughterhouse that I grew to respect the duties of certain, certain . . ." I faltered. I remembered Elida's admonition to her grandmother to behave.

"He means carrion beetles, Mama. They clean up the dirty work. Absolutely essential to life."

"And how long were you in the butchering, professor?"

"Less than a month."

"And then?"

"I quit. I went to school. I started night classes to improve myself."

"Your English is so good."

"Because the structure is similar to Dutch. And some German." I suddenly heard Cora's composed voice: *You have hardly the trace of an accent.*

"I took classes, too," Mrs. Hernandez continued. "How did you pay for it?"

"Parking cars."

"From that to the university. I cleaned apartments. And now I work for the city. Congratulations!" Mrs. Hernandez beat her boxer's fist on the table. "Now we are a success. And now you encourage my daughter. Even if I don't understand what she's doing. Study is what is important. Hard work brings luck. A chain of luck. Thank you, professor. I almost forgot to thank you."

"No, no, please don't. Elida doesn't require much encouragement."

"He means he wishes I would just get on with it, and graduate."

"I'll be very proud of her, professor, when she gets her degree. Her father, *en paz descance,* would also have been proud."

"He would have reason to be."

Elida was still picking at the bones on her plate. Something about her bent, embarrassed posture almost convinced me that I had, to some small, unexpected extent, earned my place at dinner that night. I flushed with the wine. Though a sliver of my consciousness was still hanging back, surprised, staring up at a blood-dripping conveyor belt swinging with shanks of beef.

It had been so long since I had thought about that raw, inarticulate time. So long since I'd swept blood and hair toward the drains with a metal broom, and hosed down the floor, and once reached down to pull a piece of severed calf's tongue from my shoe. Perhaps I would have been visiting somewhere else, on this Christmas Eve, drinking beer and playing poker, if I had been able to hold my own against the two union men, Polish-Americans, who'd jumped me, as if they'd learned what I'd descended from.

"What kind of name is Tristan?" Mrs. Hernandez roused me. "It sounds like *triste* in Spanish."

"It's just an old name." I cleared my throat, hoping to change the direction of this. "And your husband? He's no longer with you."

"Rogelio. No, no." She held her fist to her chest and breathed deeply. "But he's watching us tonight, I believe."

"My father was killed in an earthquake," Elida said, tipping more wine into her glass. "Years ago."

"I'm sorry. I didn't know."

"I didn't expect you to."

What did that mean? "How long ago was it?"

"Nineteen eighty-five. I was ten. We went back to Mexico City, just the two of us, to visit my grandmother. She was sick with cancer. I was the only grandchild she'd never seen. Not my *abuelita*, here. My father's mother. We were in the Juarez Hospital when it hit."

"I remember that hospital! The pictures."

"A lot of people do. But I don't really remember much of anything except the building shaking. They say it was more than a day before they pulled us out. We lost my father and grandmother both. Don't cry, Mamacita. I won't talk about it anymore."

"I'm not." She crossed herself and then held her fist to her chest again. "He'll always be here with us."

"I'm terribly sorry." I looked down at my plate. Remembering well the smell of a building when it imploded, the dust hanging in the air in the ghost of its shape. "It must have been terrible for all of you. Do you ever go back"—I turned carefully to Mrs. Hernandez—"to visit the city?"

"Never. It's too difficult. I couldn't imagine it. I won't go there again. Did you ever go back to your homeland?"

"Only once. For the same reason. To see my mother in the hospital."

"We travel for the dead or the dying. Not for the living."

"That is sometimes true, Mrs. Hernandez."

"It's the wrong idea."

"You think we shouldn't?"

"Traveling for the dying is dangerous. It only brings on bad luck. Look what happened to my husband, and almost to my little one, here."

"My mother's Mexican version of bad karma," Elida whispered.

"But traveling for the living is—by comparison—rewarding?" I asked incredulously.

I had picked up my napkin and started to refold it. Something wasn't sitting quite levelly in my stomach. I thought it best simply to bury the unwell feeling under a show of emphasis. "Because it might be," I said, speaking into my lap loudly, so loudly that some of the children in the other room stopped their games and stared at me, "it may be that traveling for the living is the much greater risk. Even *more* unlucky. Only think of it. We have too many expectations of the living. And *they* have too many of *us*. It isn't right. It's not always possible—sometimes—there can be misguided attempts, after all, but what is clear is that . . ." And as I wedged the napkin into my lap, bracingly—I don't know how it happened—I must have caught the edge of the tablecloth when my hand came down, or with my elbow, or my wrist, or my cuff links, but all at once I felt the weight of a dozen place settings and glasses and bowls and pitchers and gravy boats hurtling toward me—and when I looked up everyone's dinners had leapt and landed a foot in my direction.

The Hernandez family sat startled, looking at me.

Elida took advantage of the silence. "Neat trick!"

"Tristan," I stammered. "My name. It *is* like *triste*. It does mean sadness. You can see— Forgive me. I seem always to be—"

"And how did you get it?" Mrs. Hernandez asked helpfully, along with everyone else pulling her plates and cutlery back.

"My mother gave it to me."

"Well. Now you have everyone's attention"—she smiled expectantly—"go on."

CHAPTER

19

MY MOTHER, left at the docks by my father with nothing more than a pat on the arm and a spinster's cast-off rosary in her hand, must have looked pale as she trudged back through the Rotterdam streets. She would always say, turning the story over like a polished stone, that she knew God was testing her, to see if she had the will for life. If she had the *stomach* for it. She vowed that she did. She grew even more confident when her belly began to stick out. By her own admission, she did the only thing she could think of to do. She went to pay a visit to my father's father.

The interior of the four-story house on the formerly upper-class street was nothing like she'd imagined. Its rooms were dark, and the furniture old, ugly and chipped. My grandfather, she would learn later, had made the mistake of investing heavily in Russian currency and Russian Imperial Railway stock. Unfortunately his assets had been shot and killed, chopped up into manageable pieces, and thrown down a mine shaft. Like the Romanovs, he was never able to recover.

So it was a bitter, dying man who stared my mother up and down.

"So this is how my son proposes to rescue our fortunes," he spat at her. "By impregnating a German cow."

Perhaps the blunting of my mother's sensibilities began on this day. Perhaps she could even feel one of her heart valves shutting, like one eye in the face of a stinging wind. Her voice went as cold as a lake.

"I'll go to the police," she announced. "I'll tell them I was forced. I'll make a terrible scandal. I *was* forced." How much easier it was to aim with one eye closed.

My mother and father were hastily married by proxy a month later. My grandfather then made it clear to her he would have nothing more to do with either one of them.

"Drop dead," she told him. He was in his coffin three weeks after he had shunted her onto a boat for the East Indies.

My paternal grandmother also died in that year near the beginning of the Depression. From records I've been able to access—my highly bureaucratic homeland has always kept detailed accounts of the lives and movements of its citizens, this tidy habit making it easier, in the end, for the Nazi Party to identify its friends and enemies—it appears she suffered a stroke and had to be settled in a nursing home. After her death, my grandmother's belongings were sold off to pay bills, and what little was left put into storage. Among the few things waiting for my mother and father when they returned, beaten, from the Dutch East Indian colonies, was a blackened pine sewing table.

STANDING ON DECK as a bride, my mother knew only that she and her faraway lover were at last free to be together. In letters my father had written her he had said there would be nothing to worry about. The Indies were his oyster, waiting to be cracked open. He would soon show everyone he didn't need their help, now that he was a businessman, and independent, and soon to be a father. And so my mother stood and gulped down the sea air and made her plans. Anything could happen, after all, in a blank unknown world. People grew rich. Or died. Or they pulled themselves up by their bootstraps. Or they sank. Or they built houses. Or they were attacked by poisoned dart–wielding natives. Or they were saved.

She imagined herself as a coffee baroness. Ordering a maid to oil the hinges on a door. *No, you perfect idiot, it's still creaking!* This would have been when she wasn't sick and vomiting up potatoes over the second-class rails.

Meanwhile, the heat was unbearable, and the days wore on like a pot that wouldn't come to a boil. And the sloshing water inside her matched the sloshing and churning water under the boat, until she was convinced that, in spite of her constant Hail Marys and Our Fathers, she hadn't been absolved of her sins but was being given a sickening preview of Purgatory. Still, even she was surprised when, coming down the gangway with her knees so weak they melted like butter, my father wasn't waiting at the docks to meet her. Even she was surprised that she had to hire a rickshaw to take her to the address he had sent in his last letter. And even she was unprepared when she found him in bed with a maid. By my mother's account, my father jumped up from the native girl's legs and explained he'd misunderstood the time of her arrival.

When my sister was born in that termite-infested bungalow four months later, my mother named her Isolde, for ruined love. My father could do nothing. When I was born, three years later, I was called

Tristan. I was, apparently, an especially irritable baby. I drove my father into fits. He collapsed with malaria, lost hearing in one ear, and eventually his place at the sugar factory—where he had failed, in any case, to rise above the level of bottom-rung clerk. The four of us were then shipped back to Rotterdam. I was still so small, my mother said, I clung to her breast like a fly to a spigot.

⟗

W HEN A M AN has caused a gross disturbance in the middle of a dinner party, he has no choice but to turn himself, like this, into a spectacle. I hoped the Hernandez family would at least accept something of this as an explanation, a clumsy excuse for my clumsiness. I was careful to omit the more indelicate details.

"My mother's revenge came in our names, you see."

"Wow. Unhappily ever after," stared Elida.

"I don't understand." Mrs. Hernandez's eyes widened even farther. "Who is this Tristan and Isolde?"

"Famous unlucky lovers," I explained.

"Like Romeo and Juliet?"

"A bit more convoluted."

"There were two Isoldes." Elida, ever the scholar. "And Tristan was a knight."

"Where is your sister now?" Mrs. Hernandez asked politely.

"She's no longer living."

"That's too bad. It's all very sad. Very sad! But now I see why you were saying, why it's sometimes better to travel for the dead. At least the dead don't spill your heart's blood."

"Because the dead can't make mistakes," Elida said.

"Because the dead lack judgment," I said.

"Hey," Abuelita shouted across the table. "Would you rather travel for a funeral, or a wedding?"

"No jokes!" Mrs. Hernandez snapped at her, suddenly impatient. She shook her boxer's fist.

"I don't know, *señora*. I don't really travel much anymore, now that I'm older." I apologized, beginning to stand. It was time to excuse myself from them, en masse. I was ready to extricate myself from this odd evening.

"Well, at least you came as far as Brooklyn," Elida said as we walked to the door.

"It was nice of you to include me."

"Remember, it was to do me a favor."

"Yes. Why do you keep insisting on that?"

"I'm pretending it's your Christmas gift to me. I'm entrapping you. Forcing you to participate in common human rituals of exchange."

"Yes. But why?"

"Because you keep forgetting, Martens. We're human."

SHE WAITED WITH ME on the street, her breath trailing in a white scarf over her shoulder. I hoped I had at least acquitted myself professorially enough, in her eyes. There was nothing more I could do now, in any case. She had insisted on calling a taxi for me, saying I looked "whipped"—but this was a small indignity compared to the larger embarrassment of earlier in the evening: like a cut lip after falling in the street.

"I hope your mother can fix the gravy boat," I apologized again.

"It wasn't anything expensive. Just Woolworth china." She balanced momentarily on the heels of her boots. Blinking down, almost coy, at her raised black toes. "For me it was nice to have something out of the ordinary happening this year."

Clearly it was time to reassert the proper hierarchy between us.

"I insist you get a flight soon after the holidays."

"I will."

"I'll message over my credit card number."

"I can't ever thank you enough—"

"I'm not hearing that. I don't want to see your face again until you've become more decisive, completed some appropriate revisions, and made clearer progress altogether."

"All right. I hear you. I hear you."

No more balancing childishly on heels.

Now I could be satisfied, as the cab pulled away from her frowning face, that I had given her a stern kick in the right direction. I had done at least what was within my faltering powers to do. I had been commanding.

Of course I was a bit disoriented, on the ride home, not being familiar with my surroundings, and feeling strangely ringing and hollow after all the noise and hubbub of the night. I hadn't planned to get in so late. Outside my building, the sidewalk was strangely deserted. The single shadow hovering nearby belonged to a panhandler, a young, filthy man, clinging against the stone wall, dreadlocked, skeletal, scantily dressed. Before he could approach me, I gave him all the change I had in my pocket. And remembered how the holidays can make one feel like a vandal.

CHAPTER

2 0

FOR SEVERAL NIGHTS AFTERWARDS, unable to sleep.

At my age, could what I was experiencing be cogently described as love?

Careful. Careful. The human mind can be so easily deceived.

What had once sealed my parents together like scalding wax—was that love? Or only its painful aftermath. And what of the rudimentary shelter Agnes and I had shared? And the choiceless ties that bound families together?

A property's qualities must be understood before the property itself can be fully identified. There will be errors, inevitably, throughout the rendering of any complex process. I turned to a place on my pillow that was less saturated by my own thickened breathing. And yet, and yet, the blastedness of growing old was that so many errors had already been compounded along the way (dead father, dead mother, dead sister, lost wife, lost son) that the heart grew sick, the mind doubtful, mistrustful of itself. And so over my hunger, my yearning for Cora Lowenstein, my brain flitted, fretfully: Does one individual ever truly love another? Or is the longing really only for what one hopes to erase of oneself in the heat of the experiment?

I woke abruptly, startled in the night by my sleeping arm falling against my face.

I BECAME ANXIOUS and unglued, consumed by thoughts of her. By the need, even if she wasn't in the room with me, to look in the mirror and arrange my clothes and lift my sagging chin. To comb my remaining hairs until they fell into something like camouflage. To cut my nails, floss my teeth, gargle with mintwash. To walk as tentatively as a man in small shoes and a tight coat ready to burst at the seams. I was too uncertain, yes, unwilling to affirm what it was that was beginning to nudge us like two turtles out of the sand; but I knew, at least, this much: that when I was with her the pain drained away from my legs, by degrees, and my stomach settled, unaccustomedly; that I was able to sit still, sometimes for hours at a time; that I could even believe, though I might never, never, never actually bring myself to it, that if I wanted to I could unburden myself to her, all my sins, into the folds of her glowing ears—and that she would still try, as she often insisted, to "be decent," and a "real friend."

We walked Sandor's dog together under the stripped skeletons of the trees in Central Park, both of us bundled in scarves to our noses. When the wind blew up, we turned away from the lake, inward toward each other like two stiff figurines inside a mechanical clock, and I stood so close I could see the tear ducts in the corners of her eyes. On other dates we went together to chamber music events. A St. Valentine's concert at the university. Bach. The music neither fused us passionately, nor came between us, but executed, well behaved, over our heads, both of us sitting calmly while huge beads of sweat glinted on the brow of the cellist nearest us. "Always something so calamitous about live performances," Cora whispered to me afterwards. As we pushed through the lobby her fingers rested for a moment under my elbow, so lightly my jacket didn't even compress; and I thought of the way certain water weevils know instinctively to glide, not on the surface, but clinging to the underside of the plane of a murky pond.

I began to stop by the Chelsea Building to take her to lunch. I didn't go up the stairs or the elevator—I didn't dare—certain that if I came in close proximity again to my mother's table I would lunge for it and begin babbling like an oracle, heedless. We met instead at the first-floor entrance, in front of the chandelier shop. If our date was for dinner, it was understood that we would both pay. We might share a cab afterwards, or each drift in our separate directions. One night, coming out from a lantern-hung restaurant into an alley alive with firecrackers, we turned a corner in time to see a young Chinese-American couple celebrating their New Year by groping in the dark. I steered Cora to where she could catch a taxi, then walked to the subway and rode home. In my mind's eye I saw the Chelsea Building in ruins. Yes. It could happen. A freak foundational failure. A collapse in the early morning hours, and no one hurt but every stick and piece of furniture inside it, including one criminal table, crushed and pulverized into spume and ash.

I knew she still went regularly to visit Sandor in Connecticut. But she didn't ask me to accompany her again.

Instead, she telephoned my apartment late one weekend.

"Where are you?" I asked happily.

"At home. I was going to stay in all day and be quiet. Then, I don't know, I felt something annoying me."

"What was it?"

"Your chair."

"My chair?"

"Do you know you've never asked me to come up and see what you've done with it?"

"You were annoyed because of the chair."

"No—I'm bothered that you haven't invited me up. I'm beginning to think you must have done something horrible, Tristan."

"Like what?"

"Reupholstered it. In a terrible color. Salmon pink."

"I don't like salmon."

"That's right. I forgot. You're a herring man. You haven't redone it in herringbone, have you?"

"I haven't touched it at all."

"Then it must feel deprived." She paused. "This is where you invite me to come and see for myself, Tristan."

"I invite you to come up and look at your chair."

"*Your* chair."

"The chair."

"When would be good?"

"In about an hour?"

"Make us some tea, all right? I'm cold. We'll hang around and gossip for a change. Do you know any gossip?"

"Not really."

"We'll come up with something. Should I bring Rumford?"

I held the receiver away from his barking. The thought of his silver bell, jangling up and down my hallway, of his nails grating against my hardwood floors, of the newspapers I would have to put down . . . No. There are limits to what a man can endure.

"I'm not really pet-prepared, here."

"I'll come without him then. Can I bring anything else?"

"Not that I can think of."

"In an hour then."

And now: what frenzy. What stuffing of wrinkled pajamas into the hamper, remaking of the sheets, lowering of the toilet seat, cleaning out of the kitchen, wiping the surface of the dining table (its scratched glass spotted everywhere with my fingerprints and haloed with the ghosts of medicine-bottle caps and Pepto-Bismols and blotted and Rorschached with coffee rings and spills). And then, the problem of the chair to confront. The chair! It was still sitting, unlikely, at the end of my row of kitchen cabinets. Unhighlighted. Not the best way for Cora to see it. I hung fire, facing the door. By this time she was already buzzing downstairs.

Must act. Quickly.

I rolled my desk chair away and brought the antique to take its place. It would be difficult to explain, perhaps, how it was possible to work against such a stiffly woven back. Particularly since I had told her I hadn't intended it for such mundane use. But I would manage. I would cling as I had been for weeks. Precariously.

She smiled as I opened the door. She was patting her damp cheeks.

"I took the stairs."

"You look glowing."

I caught the suppressed flicker in her eyes as she scanned my home. The twist of her long, elegant wrists inside her raincoat pockets, as though she was having to hold them down to keep from putting things to rights.

"Eclectic mid-twentieth-century stuff," she said. "And what lovely creatures!"

"It's an old collection. I really don't keep up with it anymore."

"But they're extraordinary, aren't they?" She waded more deeply into my room. This was like watching a graceful crane pick through a littered lot. "Although . . ." She brought her pointed profile closer to the case on my wall. "I think these would give me nightmares. The giant ones, certainly. Are these your specialty?" Her breath sparkled against the *Cassidinae*. "They're so strange. They look like helmets."

"The subfamily is known for its turtle-ish appearance."

"Give me the title of one of your more obscure articles. I might want to look it up."

"'Notes on *Plagiometriona clavata*.'"

"Sounds wonderful."

"It helped me to keep my job, at one point."

"And look what you've done with your chair!"

"You see. It's the centerpiece."

"How nice. But you're not going to tell me you actually work long hours sitting in it?"

"I do. Well"—I hesitated—"that is, I have. I put it there recently because I like it, and in any case I don't work as much as I used to. Can I get you something from the kitchen now?"

"Not just yet. I'm still browsing."

"Let me take your coat."

"It's hard to believe everything you have in here. It's like standing inside a curio box."

"You don't like it."

"No, I do. It suits you."

"It's mostly relics."

"Yes, but straightforward ones. Unsentimental. Like you."

"I have sentiments, Cora."

"I know it."

"How do you know it?"

"Because I have them too. Organization is merely a function of keeping disorganization hidden."

We stood on opposite sides of my desk, wavering.

"You can't be comfortable wearing that wet thing, Cora. Let me take it."

"All right." She began unbuttoning her coat. Then stopped. Something was dragging her fingers away.

"What's that?"

She was pointing to a black-and-white sheet of paper sticking out from under the sheaf beside my computer. It was the copy of a photograph I had located only that morning at an archival website created by a Dutch university. In my hurry I had forgotten to—I must have forgotten to—I must have—

The pressure in my eardrums dropped.

"Hitler Youth," I said.

"I see that."

"National Socialist Youth," I corrected, reaching out, out to explain, but she had already pulled the image from the stack and was holding it away from me, shaking it clear now, holding it squarely, like a tablet in front of her, straightening its lineup of crisp young girls, all with their arms raised sharply, their mouths oval, shouting, operatic, above white necks and white shirts, each rigid sleeve decorated with a triangular black patch.

My hand fell back.

"That was taken in Holland."

"And why are you looking at this?"

"It's part of my research."

"Not all beetles."

"Not this."

"Why?"

"Because I have to."

"Why?"

"Because my sister was one of them."

Cora looked at me. In the same way I have seen women gaze at their children as they struggled for the first time across the drowning end of a swimming pool. The way I had seen Agnes watch Christopher while he thrashed. One part of her surprised that she still had the capacity to be hopeful. The other by how prepared she had been, all along, for him to lose the air and founder and sink out of sight.

"You're going to explain?"

"Yes. Can you sit down? Can I take your coat now?"

She didn't answer. She was still dripping. The heat on my thermostat was set at eighty degrees.

"But you will sit?"

She nodded and took one end of the sofa. I balanced on the other. This was terrible. I couldn't measure the space between us. It was so little, and yet more than I could divide into increments.

"This isn't going to be easy to talk about with you, Cora."

"I don't think I'm asking for every detail." Her voice was calm and collected, as before. As always. But no longer tolerant. No, not that. "I don't think I want to know the details. You were one of—those—too?"

"No. I was too young."

"Is that the only reason?"

"Probably. Truthfully."

"Because?"

"Because children aren't always heroes, Cora. Because—because—children generally plant the rows their parents dig."

She looked down at her fingers, spreading the joints as though they hurt her.

"I really don't need to know everything. They were collaborators, I suppose."

"Yes. My father, especially. Garden-variety drone. The lowest kind."

"So." She buried her knuckles inside her coat. "What have you been thinking about, all this time? Can you tell me that? What have you been doing? Have you been consoling yourself, somehow, with me?" She squinted now, trying not to let the light in, or to see me, or not to see me, or to hold her anger in—I didn't know. "Tristan?"

"I don't know."

"I'm still sitting here."

"I know. I'm sorry."

"You have to do better than that."

"I'm trying."

"Try again please."

"I don't know what you're willing to listen to, Cora. You once told me you wished you could be a child, because children have no decisions, no responsibility. I can honestly tell you I wasn't like those children in the picture. I wasn't pulled in. Not that way. But I can't tell you I was innocent. How could any of us have been innocent?

When I've tried—when I've wanted to, I—I was always remembering that table."

"The table?"

"The one in your store."

"You're accusing it?"

"No. I'm only trying to explain."

"About?"

"About the table."

And now it had come. I could erase a hundred lies with my next
words. I could be cut from my albatross. Or rather, I would be the
dead bird cut. Left to sink, sink, sink forever from the soothing company and surface of her green eyes.

Or I could linger a moment longer.

"I can't sleep at night, Cora."

"I don't doubt it."

"I've been wanting to tell you—"

"Why didn't you?"

"I've been wanting to tell you something. Please. Listen to me.
The phrasing in Dutch, under the table. *Als de Joden weg*— It's am-
biguous, it can mean completely the opposite of something good and
hopeful, surely it has to have occurred to you—"

"Stop it. Stop. I don't want to know. I don't want to hear it. And
now you're suffering. I never wanted that, Tristan."

"I don't know how to—"

"You simply stop. Stop right there. You're a good man. A real
friend. You have to be." She twisted her hands inside her coat.

"It's not suffering." I shook my head. "Not that."

"What then?"

"Living too long with—living without—"

"Tristan, I need to tell you what I'm thinking."

"I know. That you've been blindsided."

"No. Just this. Don't talk to me about living too long. Do you understand? Show me that much courtesy, at least. At least don't forget what you know. We've agreed to be friends. Don't find ways to insult me and mine."

"That was never my intention—"

"I don't know what your intentions were. I only know I came with the idea of having a cup of tea, and now I'm trying to remember that."

"Should I—should I put the kettle on?"

"And then you imagine we'll talk about something else?"

I stood, dumbly, but also with the bitterness of bile and disappointment starting at the back of my throat. "You say you don't want to know. All right. All right. I hear you."

That was it then. That was the blow. *She didn't want to know.* She would hold firm, unshakable, against the unpleasant and the deadly and the decisive.

"Make some tea." She lowered her voice. "And we'll listen to the rain."

With my back turned to her I could hardly keep my chin from wobbling. In the moment when love is given up as too difficult, or failed, something like hatred rises up. Something that makes the room go fetid and mean.

I'd lost her possibility. Her long, silver promise.

In my dreams, I had imagined her blue-veined legs tangled in mine. That my scar would not horrify her, as it had Agnes. That the blood thinners would somehow drain away and let what little cock was still left of me congeal, and that we would find in each other a blotting, comforting, shared solitude and escape, and perhaps even a brief wonder at our own, stubborn, continued existences. But there is nothing enticing about the cracked carapace of a man. When he loses his front, he puts his robe on quickly after he showers, he trusses himself up before the steam has evaporated from the mirror, he rushes covered out into the street where he's not in danger of being judged by his naked membrane, he becomes a desperate burrower, a borer, content always only to look, to look, not because he doesn't wish to possess a coveted thing, but because he doesn't have the right price in his hand.

And thus my hopes boiled down with the kettle. Dissolved under the spoon in my hand and against the rim of the cup.

What a fool, what a fool, to believe salvations happen.

I brought her the tea. And sat in one of the dining chairs across from her.

For a time, we said nothing.

At first I felt only bitter, thinking that now we would sit helplessly like this, pointlessly, indefinitely, until the leaves grew back on the trees and one or both of us noticed we had broken out in a fine layer of mold. Then she began to speak—as though speaking flowed naturally from a speechless situation—about Sandor. Speaking as though I wasn't even in the room. Or as though my being in it were an unfortunate occurrence, one which couldn't be addressed immediately. I was still bruised, bloody enough around the gums to resent her speaking against me, that way, as if I were only a kind of cave, an umbrella turned on its side, a mere echo.

His blood pressure had been sinking, she said without emphasis. His EEG showed no real improvement. The doctors were trying a new blood pressure medication. Had she mentioned it? He'd developed a minor disturbance in his bowels. Even something as slight as a bladder infection could kill him. The doctors were again asking her to consider placing a Do Not Resuscitate order in his medical file.

"And you say you can't sleep at night, Tristan."

"I said it was because of the table."

"It kept Sandor from sleeping. Did you know that? When we inherited it from his aunt, he didn't want it in the house. Not at first. It was like a curse he couldn't get rid of. No one could understand that. No one. But now—I do. It was an experience he had escaped and didn't share but was caught in by not having suffered through. He didn't want to keep it with him. But he didn't want not to keep it with him. I heard him arguing with himself. It kept him from sleeping until I took it away and got it set up at the store. But I tell you: if I believed, if I thought for one moment that it would keep him from sleeping, now, I would drag it into that room beside his bed and rest his head on it. *I would remind him of everything*—do you understand? Of the worst there is in this world. If it would let him have a choice in the matter."

"Cora."

"And now it's probably all too late."

"Please don't say that."

"I don't know what I'm saying, or thinking, really, at this moment."

"You have to stop this now."

"Stop? You mean you want me to leave?"

"I want you to stop being so calm, Cora. If I were you, I would want to break things into pieces." My voice was shaking with desire.

"You're not a destructive man."

"You don't have to be destructive to do a destructive thing."

"I feel that right now."

"How much does it matter to you?"

"Tristan, you're telling me your people did the housekeeping."

"How much does it *matter?*"

"I don't know." She seemed to turn away, inside herself. The sea of her eyes went deeper. "It explains certain things. The way you're so careful, when you speak. The way you talk about people. So carefully. I thought it was unusual."

"I'm a liar."

"You have lied."

"I said so."

"You were too young to get out of it any other way. Let's just leave it at that."

"I don't think I can."

"Maybe you have to."

"I can't—I'm not like you."

"You're upset, Tristan. Maybe you're seeing things far too harshly."

"Maybe I don't see how being so *reasonable* helps me!" I rose and shouted.

She stood, as surprised as I was.

I hardly recognized my own voice. I was sputtering. Angry. Confused. Yet inside the whirl of my dismay, the needle of my brain was as fixed and steady as a top's: *If I can't tell you, then I won't take anything from you. If you are afraid to hear it and I am afraid to say it then we're always going to be on one side of the glass or the other. I can't take myself back from you if I can't touch you. This will not work. It isn't working. Something is wrong. Something is missing. This is not the way, not the way, not the way. Oh, damn everything and everyone we ever make the mistake of trying to love.*

"I think you should go now, Cora."

"Tristan—"

"Please. I have to get back to work."

"You have to—get back—to work?" She turned, uncertain, steadying her eyes against the corners of the room. "All right. I'll go then. But this isn't the end of the world. I want you to know that. It isn't your fault. None of it. It can't have been."

"You're a good friend." I went with her to the door.

"But a friend isn't enough?"

"No."

"Nothing is ever what we expect, is it?"

"No, it isn't."

"I'm going, for now. Just for now. I think the dog needs a walk. It's late."

"Yes. I understand."

"No, you don't. You're a good man, Tristan. You must be. Maybe there are limits to what you can do about anything else, at this point. We all just have to live with circumstances as they are. So I'll go, and walk the dog, and we'll talk about it later."

"I don't want to talk about the dog."

"You know I didn't mean that. I'm not so small."

So quickly can a lock click, a window rattle, a dream collapse. When Cora was gone, I stood in the ruin all around me, trying to remember the things I had once, incredibly, planned. If only we human beings bore in mind more often how little the mechanical chances and outcomes of the universe take us into account, we would be less inclined toward optimism or pessimism, and more toward genuine stupefaction.

2 1

I DIDN'T ASK my mother to watch me board ship when, at seventeen, I left for this country. America. I knew she wouldn't want to face the moment—to stand and wave, and see me off—that it would irritate her, putting her too much in mind of my father escaping in the same way, twenty years before. Instead, I let her bless me in the hallway of our run-down building, then watched as she turned and went back inside, into the room where my father sat, as he always did by then, humped, brooding, with his back to the door. His last words to me were,

"Take that trash out with you."

While I made my way to the docks I couldn't shake the echo of that voice, or the image of his back, or of my mother's, crouching beside him, bending to massage his fingers, using tweezers to dig the copper splinters out that were the mark of his job at the wire works, the only factory that would hire him after he'd finished his prison term. I tried banishing their faces by staring at my tightly laced shoes as I climbed the gangway, then at the dull cleanness of my spartan berth below the ballast line. I climbed up into the fresh air again and, when the whistle sounded, leaned against the stern while the ship cast off her ropes and edged away from shore like a cut log rolled from a forest.

I vomited crossing over. I cursed. By that time, I no longer prayed. I forced myself, at moments, to remember and thank the strangers who were sponsoring me, their good deed for the year. Had I known I would soon be sweeping up blood and slipping on the extrusions from cow's entrails I would have thrown up even more of my stew. But I didn't. I held what I could down, and sucked in my breath, and told myself that, whatever the fear and uneasiness, it was a good thing to be out, to be free, to have had one's name pulled from a list. To be among the chosen.

We came around by the statue with her raised torch. I didn't expect the city to look so gray. At that hour, before dawn, even now, the island looks like a fire waiting to be lit.

MY FATHER DIED OF CANCER ten years after I emigrated. My mother didn't write to tell me about this until after his corpse had been feeding bone beetles a month in the ground. When she contracted a nearly identical cancer, ten more years later, she didn't summon me to her side until she was almost, in her words, "in God's trunk."

I went back in time to see how the ruddiness had drained from her face. How only her hands were left living things. Transparent, crawling forward like spiders along the bedsheet when she saw me.

"Tristan." She opened her eyes, blinking. "How you've changed."

"You too." I kissed her mechanically and sat.

The sallowness of her skin made her look like a mummy. Her once-dark hair was so thin I could see through its veil to her scalp, to the pillowcase.

"You stay, and bury me with Papa and Isolde," she said after she had told me again a few of the grievances of her life. "Don't send me back to Germany, to the farm. Don't put me down with the cows."

"Do the doctors say how well you're doing?"

"They know nothing. They are stupid here in these nursing homes. They keep me here and watch me like a circus. No privacy. Again. Never any privacy, since after the war. I don't even have our things from home anymore. I had to sell everything. Even Papa's watch. No inheritance for you, boy. Nothing."

"It's all right, Mama." I patted her hand with my own. "Are you comfortable enough?"

"There are these tubes. There is too much pain. It hurts from my collarbone down. Like they're putting me through a meat grinder."

"Mama."

"God is not punishing me. God is testing me, to the last minute. Like He always has."

"Would you like anything?"

"I wanted you to come. I sent you a telegram."

"I know. I'm here. Is there something else?"

"The priest has been to see me."

"What are—" I struggled to retrieve the words in Dutch. "The painkillers. That they're giving you?"

"Some drug, I don't know."

"Does it help?"

"When they give it. I don't want to talk any longer, now. I'm tired. I've told you everything. It's enough now that you're here. But God Almighty, this pain. Even your father didn't have so much suffering. I'm glad you didn't see him like that. I'm glad you didn't come, then. He wouldn't have liked you to know he was such a waste of a man. All this dying, it's got nothing to do with you anyway. You're an American. The only one in the family. Stay that way. Stay healthy. You shouldn't come here. Why have you?" She began to stir, agitated. "Why did you come here?"

"You sent me a telegram, Mama."

"How did you get here?"

"An airplane, Mama."

"You go home to your wife. You bury us all together, and then you go home to your good, healthy wife."

"And my son. I have a son, Mama. Your grandson. I sent you pictures, remember? Christopher."

"*Ja,* " she said vaguely. That was her final word to me. She closed her eyes, and after a moment her hands loosened on the heavy pewter rosary at her chest. She slept. I called for the nurse to come in. Later, in the evening, she died. I made all the necessary arrangements.

I wandered around the city the next day. Rotterdam was almost unrecognizable. Gone were the vacant lots, the deep craters that had lingered long after the bombings, the blackened facades of the old buildings. The sagging, horse-drawn carts filled with ash. The shells of the burned-out churches, the piles of rubble standing on the corners. The city was now modern. Sleek and psychedelic. On the streets businessmen brushed past hashish vendors. The skyline was so sharp it was like the sketch of a new city. The new, geometric apartment houses were of steel and concrete, tilted playfully, like cubes in a glass (I thought of Christopher at home in his crib, sucking on his blocks).

A new, gleaming bus carried me out to the old neighborhood. But our wartime flat was no longer standing. No reason to expect it to be. Our row of houses had been replaced by a large, brown, cinderblock building filled with East Indians and Surinamese. I stood across the street and watched them string laundry from their windows. The air was spiked with curries. I turned and followed a wet breeze until I was at the harbor again, and came out at a slanting network of new docks. Here, too, all was bright and unrecognizable: the massive cranes, the monster derricks. The dregs of older, smaller docks and fallen piers were left to rot to one side, sticking like ribs out of the water.

Here Isolde and I, in the months just before the war, had played together. Here we had screamed at gulls, and thrown coffee beans at them, and hidden behind barrels that smelled of decaying fish. Here I had learned to doubt and admire my sister, both, the way all younger siblings do, watching the older one reach farther and faster and more energetically. The memory of her bare, white, golden-flecked arm hung in the air tracing a kind of script in front of me, but the emotions it conjured were all contradictory, admiration and envy, trust and fear, partner and competitor, love and hate.

ON QUIET, CLOISTERED SUNDAYS we sneaked into the empty wharf houses, and on our hands and knees picked through the dust and woodshavings in the corners and in the damp earwigged cracks along the walls, prying leftovers from the holds of ships. Cinnamon sticks. Shining nails. Clumps of raw tea. Tortoiseshell buttons. Dried apples. Sewing needles. Pipe tobacco. Twined hemp. Beetles lay dead, dropped in circles where sacks of grain had been rolled away. The shipping clerks had dropped their stubbed pencils. We picked them up. We were the lowest scavengers on the turf. We bruised ourselves, looking. And we collected everything that could be saved.

There were ordinary school days, after Isolde came home, when we went down to watch the dockmen load and unload crates. One cloudless afternoon when a shipment of India rubber came through. A crane swung a huge raw pink ball out from the hold in a slow pass.

"What would happen if it fell?" Isolde chewed her green apple into my ear and nudged me.

"What would happen?" I answered.

Instantly, the rubber broke from its net. It lengthened like a finger, and then plunged and hit the dock, once, making a thick, warbling sound, like a bell ringing underwater. Then it bounced as high as a steeple in the air, soaring beautifully, fantastically against the sun.

"Look." Isolde pointed.

It bounced again, and again, and again, and then once more, only, crushing a newspaper kiosk and rolling down the wharf, turning over barrels, knocking out light posts. I stared up at my sister, wide-eyed.

"It's all done now," she said.

Later she would tell me not to whine so much or ask to see it again. Our new friends the Germans, after all, were very strict about rubber.

～

AFTER CHECKING on my mother's funeral arrangements I followed the old, irregular streets out to that part of Rotterdam where the families of war criminals, like mine, had been kept during and after the trials. My mother lay slack-cheeked in a morgue. My father was now a carton of bones and dust. I had become—and not merely geographically—an orphan. But none of this felt new to me; none of it seemed to be an occasion for shock, or surprise, or even a mild shift in awareness. My heart beat dully and methodically as I walked on. My palms were cold, as they had been in the mortician's office. If an obscure, run-down hotel still had the power to make me shiver with dread, I ignored this. I drew closer, and now it became clear that this particular street, like so many others, had been refurbished. Which meant that very likely the building would be gone, too, torn down to make way for a parking lot or a brewery.

But no. There it rose, in front of me. Its facade thoroughly restored. The entire block surrounding it had already been converted into pleasant shops and sidewalk cafés. People were coming and going and lounging in the salty breeze, comfortable, nonchalant, aloof and watchful, in the old stout Dutch way—as if there had never been crimes and punishments, escapes, or forcible returns. Even the walkway leading me forward looked the same, and the front door, and the brass plate, though cleaned and polished so thoroughly I could see my reflection bulging inside it.

I passed in. A maître d' bowed and arranged a table for me by the windows, with a view of the harbor. The lobby was now part of the restaurant. A young waiter held his hands behind his back, his shoulders tipped at an angle, ready to take my order. He probably knew nothing about the terms that had been served there. I tried imagining telling him that I had once spent three years of my life scraping and repainting the windowsills upstairs, while my mother, with the other prisoners' wives, muttered and spat and scrubbed some of the tile he was standing on.

"*Mijnheer?*" He bowed.

I ordered coffee, black. My hands seemed to float above the white tablecloth, unable to land. There is a sensation, when you return to a well-known place that has changed completely, of being not quite at home in yourself. As though in stripping away outer layers of paint and brick and mortar someone has stolen your clothes and cleaned them and brought them back to you shrunken and stiff. My chest felt tight.

Somewhere above me was the apartment where we had waited out my father's three-year sentence: the two, stark, high-ceilinged, sparsely furnished rooms from which I had gone out, in whatever thin coat my mother was able to patch together for me, to school, where the "ordinary" children shunned or taunted me, and I was left to make friends with the gutters. And somewhere above, too, was the windowsill at the end of our floor, the fifth, where my sister on that first day had already decided she'd had enough, and set her foot, and shouted, and flew out.

"*Mijnheer?*"

"*Bedankt.*"

The waiter poured my coffee.

"Excuse me—but what can you tell me about this old hotel, please?"

"We're a full-service establishment, sir. There is a spa here, and also a roof terrace." He was a simple, ordinary young Dutchman, tall and blond, hair shaved close, like a recruit's. The face of a northerner. The type my mother would have called "prune-fed."

"The building was recently renovated?"

"Very recently, sir."

"What was it before this?"

"Vacant for a few years, I think."

"And before that?"

"It was a transit hotel for passengers on board some of the old cruise lines. In the twenties. Very popular with immigrants, until the thirties, until the bad times, and then it closed down."

"Anything else?"

"Not that I know."

"Thank you."

"Someone at the front desk can show you around, if you would like it, sir."

"No, thank you," I said. "Thank you."

And what would the gray-haired women having their tea and cake, and the businesspeople sitting across from each other trying hard not to look competitive, and the couples snaking their hands past the silverware and twining their fingers into lovers' knots—what would they have done, what would they have said, if I had stood up and described exactly how we had gotten here, and the way things had been, in the end, for us?

Probably, "You got what you deserved, or maybe less. Too bad."

The Dutch, I should explain, are a tolerant but not particularly forgiving race. At least not more so than the rest of humankind. I know this.

T H E   R E P A T R I A T I O N   O F F I C E R S had found us in my mother's old village, on a tip. It was their job to track down traitors who had fled to Germany. By the end of 1945, they knew not only where most such people were, but what exactly they felt like doing with us. A truck came to my aunt's farm, and we were loaded onto the back of it. My father first—with the only bag we were allowed to carry. My mother next, jerking my sister by the elbow, pulling her roughly in, because it was her fault we'd all been caught. And me, last, helped up by an older man I didn't recognize. Twenty of us were squeezed in and standing exposed in the truck bed. We were brought to a train station, where a cattle car waited, and loaded as a group on to this.

I was confused; only eleven years old. I pushed and squeezed my way through to the door of the rail car and put my fingers through the slats, and peered out. I knew enough, of course, to be ashamed by the fact that we had been herded into a cattle car. I knew enough to know we were in trouble. I knew enough to concentrate on not wetting my pants. But I was also young enough to be most urgently sad because of the animals I'd had to leave behind on my aunt's farm, and for the games I would no longer play, and because Isolde had finked on us.

I couldn't, then, see the connections that were being made. The rocking of the car was both harsh and soothing. No one could tell me where we were going. We were simply moving. Nothing at all had happened yet. The feeling of standing and bouncing over each iron seam stayed with me even after we had been routed out onto the platform at Westerbork.

I was separated from my mother and sister then and sent with my father to a processing area, where we were told to remove our clothes, showered with large, cold hoses, and then blasted with DDT. Now I was frightened. All around me were naked men and boys, hunched, whimpering, coughing, spitting, cupping their genitals between their legs. We were given our clothes back and put in lines and handed papers and then sent off to sleep in a barracks. On our way out a group of emaciated, weeping men followed and cursed us, shouting, until we were safely inside the building.

In a stiff hour before dawn I was pulled to the floor by my father, then tugged back to the moonlit station platform, where my mother and Isolde stood morose, delousing powder still caked around their necks. I slept on the hay inside the train. When I woke again my father was no longer with us and we were being pulled off and loaded into an ambulance with three other women and two children. The van brought us to the former transit hotel; at first I was afraid it was a hospital. We were handed more papers and a key, and told we would have to find our own meals that day.

My mother was allowed to visit my father three times during his trial, and once a month afterwards, at the labor camp. She didn't describe it in detail, except to say that there was too much barbed wire, too many guards shouting, three roll calls a day, and bad food.

⁓

STANDING AT THE GRAVE SITE and facing the plot—seeing my father's name, and Isolde's name again for the first time in twenty years, and the newly dug hole that would be my mother's—I could bring myself to feel nothing. The morning wind whipped up like a wave against my back. There were hardly any people at the cemetery that day, just a few old Rotterdammers with flowers bundled in newspaper, bent and picking at the weeds, frowning, their bottom lips pushed out in regret. I wondered if I had become unnatural. I felt hard. Yet strangely light, as though filled with air. I looked at the coffin; I looked at the mound of fresh earth; I had recently looked at the mounds of African termites with more intensity and frustration. First, came a kind of relief. Then a cough, and a short spasm. I shed no tears. I was a grown man. I was married. I had a young son. I lived in the United States of America, I had become a man of education and profession and distinction. I was methodical, conclusive, decisive. I had escaped. I had made good. There seemed to be no reason, then, to think of such events anymore, or to try to stir what lay dead and buried.

2 3

EVERY TIME YOU LOOK at your son or daughter, see your own mistakes. Every time you hear your children's names, remember how you fled, and were found.

These were the curses my mother set on my father's head. When he returned to Rotterdam from the Indies, with none of the riches he'd planned to make, but poor, and helpless, and with a wife and two hungry children, and with no family or connections of any sort to call on, he must have believed himself in a kind of fever-induced trance. He must have waited, incredulous, disoriented, to wake up. But a new morning didn't come. By the time I was old enough to remember him, he was already a gaunt man who stiffened when he heard the slightest, grating sound. He was no longer the gangling boy pictured by a motorcycle that wasn't his in the photo my mother kept on the narrow mantel above our coal stove, until my father grabbed it, one night, and stuffed it into the grate.

He was a thin, watchful man whose chin shot up whenever he was approached, like a bird swallowing a fish before it could be taken from him. Unlike my mother, he never spoke in the form of confessions or stories. Only in commands.

"Isolde, Tristan, sit down and eat."

We sat down at the oilclothed table, and ate.

"Look, you, here is something sticky on the floor."

My mother swept and mopped the warped tiles.

He made a list for her and nailed it by the door:

> Monday—laundry.
>
> Tuesday—ironing.
>
> Wednesday—clean living room.
>
> Thursday—clean bedrooms.
>
> Friday—beat rug with *mattenklopper*.

Often he had no job—and so was around to make sure things got done. My mother took his commands silently and obeyed them. My earliest memories of her are of the tension in her body while he watched her, as though I could understand, even before it was possible for me to read anything at all, the lines that were pasted across her forehead as crookedly as the seamed wallpaper pasted our flat:

See how I fulfill my role dutifully. See how you will never have any reason to complain about me. None at all.

In this way my mother made sure every demand my father shouted out echoed back to him in the form of a stinging recrimination. Still, he couldn't stop himself.

"Clean up this grease spot."

"We live in our own, orderly way," I once overheard my mother telling the neighbor in the apartment underneath ours, who'd complained about all my father's shouting and rapping on chairs and tables. "Man commands his family. God commands man."

"God is less noisy about it," the neighbor said.

We were clearly objects of pity before the war. When Isolde and I walked down our street, the women sometimes stopped to give us candy. The men looked at us kindly, and winked their encouragement, and patted our heads. A bag of oranges might break loose from a passing truck, but no one would stare when Isolde jumped from the curb to collect them in her skirt. At home we peeled and ate them under the black table, warm there because it was pulled up near the stove.

My father held two jobs briefly before the Occupation. One was selling silk hosiery. On the side he brought home stockings women had tried on and found holes in and left in the "damaged" department. My mother would darn and wash these, and then sell them cheaply on the street. My father was quickly fired, not for stealing, but when it was discovered he had sold one leg of a pair at half price to a customer who needed to replace only one stocking. He would later say that this was why the Dutch people needed the Occupation: they had become incapable of simple numerical logic.

He then tried his luck at a tobacco shop around the corner from our flat. Isolde and I were allowed to come and sit inside, away from the windows, behind the open, empty safe. We watched while he grew angry at customers who didn't buy as he advised them to, berating them for foolishly ignoring the tastes of a man who had lived in the Indies, after all, and was therefore completely knowledgeable in the field of tropical leaf-growth. One day a man in a long coat came in to pick up his box of cigars, taking out a penknife to break the seal.

"Don't be such a fool. See what you're doing!" my father told him. "You have to open it from the *other* side."

The man, in his long, warm coat, looked at my father, but didn't shift the box. Instead, he sliced along the red seam at the back meant to serve as its hinge. When he had finished this, he smiled and flipped open the top from the wrong side, took out a sample, licked his lips and put it in his mouth, and walked out of the shop.

"Do you want me to call the nuthouse now?" my father shouted after him.

My mother patched and sewed, making our clothes out of remnants and castoffs. She must have closed her eyes to our pitifulness. I went to Isolde's First Communion wearing a suit that had been cut down from a boy's twice my age, my arms and legs hanging out of the bells of the sleeves and shortpants in thin clappers. Isolde's white dress also had to be cut down, but she seemed content with the bell effect, swinging her skirt from side to side, practicing her Our Fathers. Her blond hair hung in rag curls. Her eyes were round and eager. She always loved costumes and attention.

When my father couldn't put meat on the table my mother sewed in barter, letting out the dresses of the butcher's wife, or making up a wedding veil for the cheese man's daughter. I watched the grimace on her face as she worked into the night, the skin on her knuckles worsting like the material. When her hands grew sore she sat on them until they flattened.

My father hovered over her and repeated his orders:

"Dinner by six o'clock. Don't forget to write your sister tonight. Tell them we expect to hear from them." My mother had been writing to her family in Germany for money.

"Oh, you should see it there, children. There are mountains, and white castles, and underneath them men who lie to you. It's nothing like the big flat city here. It's small and clean and dull. But the milk is free and the air smells like bees."

"How can the air smell like bees, Mama?"

"The same way it can smell here of horses and piss, Tristan."

"When do we go, Mama?" asked Isolde, squeezing her knees together in excitement.

"When God sends us a sign."

She was gruff with us—scrubbing our necks and ears at night with an abstractness I didn't understand until I saw farm animals being washed. When it was time for bed and I was still too small and afraid to go out by myself to the water closet all the families used, outside in the hallway on the landing, she would take me there, holding me by the wrist while I felt the cold boards with my feet. "Here, boy, go on. No one's inside." She would wait until I had finished. She was reasonably patient for a woman who was not, I understood later, much interested in her children, but only in the accident that had made us.

She watched my father's every move. Listened to his every cough. His bursts of gas. His growlings. She massaged his shoulders both when he told her to and when he didn't, trimmed his hair and pared his nails, turned his collars back and smoothed them down, set out his shoes, made his coffee, boiled his eggs, fried his herring. He lingered near her while she did her sewing, kept her accounts, soaked her potatoes, soaped the windows. It was as if, looking shrewdly past love, each had become the other's sharpest weapon.

"God will watch over us," my mother often said.

My father didn't go to Mass. He said religion was for women and boys.

"Don't listen to that. God will bring us into the safe harbor, children, you'll see. We'll have milk and honey in the bowls." While I sat beside my mother during Communion I looked, hunting for swarms in the rafters. But there was no sign of anything except the fixed stations of the cross circling us like birds. Isolde came back with the Communion bread between her teeth, looking down, mincing, her hands folded together piously. She said the holy wine tasted like marzipan. She loved a performance.

At home again, when I lay in my bed inside my small closet, I fell asleep by listening to her breathing in the next small room, trying to match my lungfalls to hers. In no other way could I make us identical. She was older. Taller. Stronger. She threw farther, and more precisely. She was tawny-skinned, like a lion cub; people in the street always wanted to pet her. While I was small, and dark, and pale, with pockets under my eyes that bulged like marbles. She was also smarter, and knew things—but didn't always tell me what I needed to know. When she wanted to sound superior, she acted just like him.

We sensed something when the change in our fortunes began. He came home one day, more excited than usual, with a paper rolled in his hands. He followed my mother around while she cooked, talking loudly. Isolde and I were huddled keeping warm under the table by the stove.

"I'm telling you, we're finally going to see a difference."

"Good."

"It's men like me who have suffered and seen ourselves cheated by the darker forces."

"Pass the salt."

"We're finally going to see some order. Some sanity. The politicians of this country have allowed it to become womanly and weak, negotiating with everyone. It's time for men to be men, and cowards to be cowards. I'm saying, there's no room for shirkers and thieves. It's the dawn of a new day."

"I told you it would come."

"It's here. I'm telling you. When the Jews are gone, it will be our turn."

I took a stubbed pencil from my pocket and put it between my teeth. Isolde grabbed it from me and reached up. I watched. Admiring. She was nine and could space letters squarely and evenly. I took the pencil when she'd finished, and began tracing over the words carefully, darkening and deepening them as I went, feeling my strength, pushing the thick lead up, up, up into the soft wood, claiming the letters for my own and, in my clumsiness and grinding, making them larger.

In 1938, refugees had already begun arriving from Germany. Holland's borders were soon closed.

In 1939 Holland had declared neutrality, hoping to stay out of the war. Three hundred thousand men were at that time, however, mobilized to prepare for a German invasion.

My father wasn't among them, pleading the deafness in his ear.

In April 1940, during a radio speech, Hitler assured the Dutch people that he would respect any declaration of neutrality, and that in any case Holland was a small country, unimportant to his campaign, so there was no reason for anyone to worry.

On May 10, airdromes at Waalhaven, Bergen, Schipol, and de Kooy were bombed. A ground attack enveloped the Dutch southern flank and captured the bridge across the Maas River. German paratroopers began landing on the bridges at The Hague, Dordrecht, and Moerdijk.

May 11: The French army is cut off at Breda while trying to reach the Dutch, who had fallen back from the Maas.

May 13: The French begin their retreat. The Dutch royal family flees to England. Hitler is reported to be annoyed that it has taken more than a day or two to overpower a tiny nation.

May 14: The Dutch high command gives in and begins its surrender. At 1:30 in the afternoon, however, German planes begin to speckle the skies over Rotterdam.

MY FATHER HAD KEPT Isolde home from school that day because he was convinced her teacher wouldn't explain the invasion properly to her class. We had just finished our lunches of bread and cheese when the roar shook the milk in our cups and he jumped from his chair and shouted excitedly at us to follow him downstairs. He pointed up as the planes passed overhead.

"See! It's finished! They're flying across in celebration. Look how perfect they are!"

The bombs, when they fell, at first appeared like small ribboned packages. The woman standing in front of us dropped to her knees. I thought she had stumbled and was feeling for her glasses. The howling came next, from the sky, from the ground, from the air-raid sirens, from the street as we were shoved by a rush of people screaming at us from behind. The air filled with a stench like pulverized eggs. A hole in time opened up, a hole that seemed to go down and down and down and never end. Then the ground broke again into fishlike spasming. I was being dragged by my mother, then pushed. We were back inside the house and she was shoving us under the table. I could hear her teeth grinding next to my ear. She was mumbling and praying and telling her beads on our necks, still telling us to be quiet and pray to God when my father rushed in and announced it was all right, it was over, though some of the churches and the schoolchildren in their classes had been hit, and most of the center of town. Something in his voice shrieked like a kettle my mother had put on for too long.

We lined up as the soldiers came goose-stepping into our city. I saw some of our neighbors turning away and crying, and others, people I didn't know, keeping their mouths shut and standing mutely while their eyes, broken open like flowerpots, emptied. My parents were among those who stood with one arm stiffly raised.

I was six years old. Isolde raised her arm higher than mine. But I caught the wink of an officer passing in his car. And so eclipsed her.

THE TROUBLE WITH ELECTRONIC MAIL is that it makes you feel you have no place left to hide. I glanced up, and was forced to notice the tiny envelope. Blinking.

No escape.

At least this message was short, meaning it didn't need to be printed out and rolled up and carried like a vial of nerve gas down into the subway:

Dear Dad

Greetings from the land of milk and honey. All is well here. I can't help but wonder, with the new year well under way, if this will be the season that brings you closer to your family, and closer to Christ and God the Father. I never lose hope—my faith is as firm as iron, and God's might aims as straight as bullets. I know it's only a matter of time before you see the light. So. Why don't you just come to your senses and come here and break peace and make bread [*surely one of*

us had that backwards?] with God, and us, and submit yourself
to the POWER OF HEAVEN. We never know when the Day
of Judgment will be lo nigh at hand, the earth poised on the
brink and ready to descend into chaos and madness and the
ranks of the true believers ready to be called to order. I can't
bear the thought of you being on the side of the damned,
Papa. Neither can the rest of us. It hurts us. We all send our
prayers up daily that you'll be delivered. The faithless are all
around us and the battle is just beginning. We need you.
Mama says hello, she's joined a prayer circle, by the way, and
is becoming more restful every day. Ray is fat and starting to
walk like a tank. You should see him. We look forward to
your coming down and taking your place behind us. In
Christ's blood, your loving son,

Christopher

Sometimes, I do try to imagine what life must be like for you. It
must be a torture, for you—imagining me bound for a future con-
demned to hellfire—with nothing you say unprecedented enough to
startle me. I feel badly for you, my son, I do. I do. But in such terms,
in this manner, you can't expect me to incline toward you. In fact, I
would be lying if I didn't admit that I regard you with a certain
amount of nervous dread, the way my colleagues in California regard
the Western oak bark and oak-ambrosia beetles, perfectly harmless
unless you get too many together, and then the trees start falling, too
much dry fuel is left lying around, and before you know it, acres and
acres of scorched wood . . .

The phone's ring saved me from more of this kind of maun-
dering.

"Hello?"

"You haven't called."

"I've been busy."

"You've been avoiding me."

"I thought it was the other way round."

"Meet me?"

"Why?"

"For lunch."

"I'm not hungry."

"Don't be stubborn. I'm just around the corner, Tristan. Meet me downstairs."

"You don't want to come up?"

"No,—v—go—fo—"

"You're breaking up, Cora."

"I'm on the mobile. Is that better? Meet me, and we'll just take a walk. It's starting to warm up out."

"I don't think I'm up for it."

"Indulge me."

"My groin hurts."

"Parts of me hurt, but I'm too polite to mention them."

"How soon, then?"

"Ten minutes. I'm walking your way now."

I started down in five, and found her looking up at my living room window, shielding her eyes from the sun. Then saw how she'd wandered into my neighborhood: she had Rumford with her. So now, along with other shames and awkwardnesses, I would have to resign myself to one of those aimless, meandering doggy walks with frequent doggy stops, with doggy pausings to smell barren circles of earth around the already splattered trunks of trees, with doggy jerkings of the leash away from other doggy dogs, and from the legs and heels of the hooded sidewalk vendors.

We fixed our eyes somewhere above Rumford's bald tail. I noticed something.

"Where's his bell?"

"I threw it into the lake."

"You did what?"

"I threw it—into the lake."

"Why?"

"Because it was making a happy sound, and I didn't feel so happy. So I took it off and tossed it."

"That must have been—liberating," I said vaguely. I thought it best to keep things slightly off-center between us.

"And you've been keeping busy, Tristan?"

"I had another letter from my son today."

"How is he?"

"Only a fool would try to talk to someone as mixed up as that."

"Really."

She reached down to pat the dog, and the way she spoke, levelly, told me we had reached a stage in our relationship where we would now be very direct with each other about some things, while at the same time completely elliptical about others. "Are you sure, or is that just cowardice on your part?"

"Worse than that."

"Meaning?"

"I've given up. I've decided I'm a finished parent."

"Not having children, I don't understand if that's possible." She walked on, pulling the dog at a diagonal away from a threatening Doberman. "But I am sorry for you."

"I don't feel anything at all, right now."

"With me, it's just the reverse. I'm feeling things I don't know where to put."

"Do you remember when you were young, and it seemed that there was nothing you could choose, that everything was already chosen for you, even the food on your plate?"

"Yes."

"And do you remember feeling trapped—even on the best days? Your clothes, your shoes, your coat, your house, your school, your family, the day, the night, the next day, and the next, the same shoes, the same coat?"

"Yes."

"And now, the general idea is that we can choose almost anything, at any time. Instantly ordered gratification."

"You're losing me, Tristan."

"But nothing changes. Because the options aren't real ones."

"There are some that are real."

"Not many."

"How do you know?"

"You were the one who said we were stuck with the circumstances we're given."

"Maybe I didn't mean it that way."

"I wonder who we ask to find out?"

"I had hoped it would be each other," she said, and jerked the dog's chain so sharply from a hydrant he yelped and buckled onto his chest.

She stopped, taken aback. I pulled up beside her and got the wind knocked out of me as my shoulder collided with a passerby's. The pain rang down into my gut. Like the echo of a cannon shot, it brought up a submerged dream from the night before—a nightmare, one I had been lucky enough not to remember until that moment— but now it overwhelmed me again, and I was approaching Cora's bedroom only to find her floor covered in a layer of something white—what was it? powder? flour?—which I understood would show my tracks, and so I had tried to leap over this, to her, but when I did stumbled and landed on something hard, my own fists, and tore open my nightshirt.

She was bending and apologizing profusely to the dog.

"Your cell phone is ringing, Cora."

"I don't want to take it."

"Is that all right?"

"No. I'll turn it off."

She straightened and pulled the phone from her jacket, but saw something that made her answer it. I moved away into the shade near a hot-dog cart. The smell of sauerkraut was old and unpleasant.

I watched as her face went still. Her lips were moving, almost imperceptibly. She did nothing while Rumford circled his leash around and around her, entangling her heels.

I hurried back to her side. "Something's wrong?"

She hung up.

"They're describing it as 'extreme agitation.'"

"How can that be?"

"I don't know."

"What do you want to do?"

"I'm going there."

"Of course."

"Come with me."

"How can I?"

"We'll take a cab back to my place and leave the dog, then take my car."

"No, I mean, you're sure you want me to—"

"Please. Don't make me ask again."

"Of course not. I wouldn't."

This was another sort of test, I understood. Some point that had to be driven deep into me before it could pass through.

THE WREATHS HAD BEEN PULLED from the hospital doors and colorful, springlike flowers hung up in their place. The halls teemed with nurses and orderlies and families carrying balloons and more flowers. We were kept waiting at the desk of a floor nurse because some question had to be asked, or form recovered. Then a doctor appeared, a short man who looked too young for the cleft in his chin, rubbing his right temple, acutely, as though he had been engaged somewhere in a problem of long division.

I moved off into the waiting area, to give them privacy. The murmurs were distinct enough. Complications. Husband put on ventilator for short period. Stabilized now. Off ventilator. Still in the intensive care unit.

The doctor now gestured toward the depths of the center.

"If you'll come with me, Mrs. Lowenstein, I'll take you to him."

She nodded slowly and turned.

"I'll wait," I said, almost touching her arm as she passed. A simple reflex-response.

I sat down on the upholstered bench against the wall. She wouldn't be thinking of me, now. She had grown less and less aware of me, even while we drove. Soon she would be standing over her husband's bed, over his limp, fallen, clearly outlined body; plumbed to her heels with a flood of guilt and grief. A weight so heavy on her shoulders it would seem to demand that she sink under it. Except that she doesn't sink, because one doesn't sink, under such conditions; one floats, miraculously, one looks and looks and looks, hovering, unbelieving, refusing, while before one's very eyes the other, without twitching a muscle, sinks so quickly that light and sound can't follow, can't keep pace. And then the body is put in a box and taken to the cemetery. And then one runs away between the headstones, crying.

How fast is the speed of light, Christopher?

I don't know, leave me alone. I'm going to my room. I don't care about your science crud. What does it help, anyway, knowing that crud?

In the beginning, at the start of the coma, Cora had told me, she'd had to teach herself to rise by degrees in the morning; learning again how to face herself in the mirror. First, in the early weeks, getting up before three, when it was still dark and there were no mirrors. Then, day after day, month after month, edging the clock forward, minute by minute, toward the inhuman routine; toward sunrise. Until, after more than a year, she could finally brush her teeth and open her eyes without choking on her own reflection.

Sandor had once told her a story about a Jew who had decided it was time for him to marry. His mother obligingly went out and found three brides for him: a Jew, a Christian, and an atheist. Then she told her son to give each of these women a thousand dollars, and watch to see what each one did with the money.

The atheist woman bought him gifts.

The Christian woman gave all the money to charity, in his name.

The Jewish woman invested the money, doubled it, and returned the original amount to him, plus the profit.

So which woman did the man marry?

We were sitting in her living room, under her pyramid ceiling, her palm tree fanning over our heads.

"The one he loved," Cora had said.

⟿

I HEARD A SQUEAKING of soft heels around the corner, and looked up, hoping to see her. I had been sitting for so long, an hour, almost two. My joints had dug like pikes into place. The quickening feet, however, belonged only to a small nurse with round, nutlike cheeks. She smiled and touched my sleeve.

"Are you Mr. Martens?"

"Yes?"

"I'm Padma. I've been sent to tell you the situation."

"Yes. Thank you."

"I'm glad you're sitting down."

"How is she?"

"She's good."

"And . . . Mr. Lowenstein?"

"That's why I'm glad you're sitting, Mr. Martens. Something's happened. He's spoken."

"He's what?"

"I know, it's unexpected. But he's spoken. We're still not sure what's organizing the neural—"

"But that's—that's—"

"Everything's under control, Mr. Martens. Please don't worry. We're running more tests right now."

"What did he say?"

" 'Louder.' That came first."

"And then?"

"Then Mrs. Lowenstein's name. That's a good sign. That's memory function."

"Cora."

"And he's responding to light. Mr. Martens—are you feeling all right? All this could be too much. But it does happen. I can assure you. It's okay. Can I get you something to drink? You look—"

"No. No." No. I was standing. I had to leave now, I had to go. I put my hand against the wall behind us. And yet, even then, I longed to turn toward the ICU, in that last moment, to tell her, frantically, in the last fraction before I fled, how I had loved her. But there was no time. No chance. Pointless. Pointless, now. What was love but something stuffed in the mouth so that it was impossible to breathe? Something that left a man tied by the hands and legs, unable to act, to save, to move, to admit or offer much, with his eyes wide open so that he could see the one he loved in her delight, in her hope, in her transfiguration, while at the same time there was nothing left for him to do but spit the last of his illusions out, and fall on the sword.

"Mrs. Lowenstein did ask if you wanted these."

I cringed from her. I didn't take the car keys. "No."

"You're sure you're all right?"

I looked again at that full ring. With the key that would unlock Lowenstein's Fine Antiques and Reproductions.

"Please. Just tell me how to get to the nearest train station."

CHAPTER

2 5

MY FATHER, rushing, flailing, with sweat-stains like open jaws under his arms, began locking up cabinets and shouted at us to pack what clothes and toys we could into our school bags. My mother was at the table cramming food and clothing and pieces of china and silverware into a suitcase. Isolde and I ran to look out the window. Everywhere our neighbors were draping orange banners from the roofs, from their pipes, from the casements. Our street looked ready for a parade.

By the time we came out, the mob was ready for us.

"Traitors!"

"Nazi boot-lickers! Where will you hide now?"

"Stinking NSBers!"

"Scum! Filth! Wait. Be careful—there are the children."

"Where are you going now, with your stolen things?"

"See if you can make it to Germany!"

"Murderers! Cowards! God will punish you!"

My father kept a crablike grip on my neck, facing me forward and pushing me ahead of him through the crowd and into the narrow channel left down the center of our street. We joined other people wearing layers of clothes and pushing carts or baby carriages filled with suitcases and paintings and lamps and silverware, while German soldiers with guns who seemed to be on a mission that had nothing to do with us flew by in open trucks, and an old, shabbily dressed couple hobbling together on one cane stood and balled their fists at us and wept with joy, and children cheered. I could feel my mouth open, sucking in air. My heart hammering inside me. Those orange flags were so bright, on that Tuesday.

I slipped out from under my father's grip and turned in time to see our neighbors throwing our furniture out the window, in time to see the legs of my mother's sewing table balanced on the ledge, then falling, then twisting, then disappearing and reappearing, rising and bobbing up on a bed of lifted arms, then tumbling and getting lost again in the thickness, before we were sucked and passed through a separate, roaring thickness. Gone.

2 6

TWO YEARS BEFORE we had been, as my father said, on the master's side of the table.

"And there are new positions coming open in the Party all the time, I tell you! Real opportunities!"

He'd announced this one night after blackout—while my mother cooked dinner and kept her shoulder turned to the rest of us—sitting and licking his fingers importantly over his newspapers.

"Any time now I'll be made head clerk in the rations division. You watch. And then more. All of the civil service has been cleaned up. There's room enough for the right kind of people now."

"The children are growing very fast," my mother said without looking.

"This new discipline is good for them."

"Other men bring home more extras."

"You don't know what you're talking about."

"You're right. It's never good to see more food on the table."

"I'm watched, I tell you. I'm not going to be shoved off into one of the camps."

"So many ration cards. You give out hundreds. Thousands."

"They belong to the Reich."

"Then they belong to me."

"You have no idea what you're talking about."

"Of course. You must be right."

"Cheats, thieves and cowards. I'm not part of the vermin of this world."

"Yes, it's good people who eat kale five times a week."

"Look at your new tablecloth. Look at your plates. Where do you think they come from? Look at your haircombs."

"I'll put some hair out to eat, then."

"Don't be stupid. We're investing. You have to think of it that way. We have to be forward-looking. You should hang the Führer's portrait higher, where everyone can see it from the street. And we must have another soldier in for dinner."

My father was so satisfied with National Socialism that when he wasn't at work he was busy handing out pamphlets on the street corners, or in front of the *Kringhuis N.S.B.* under the words *Volk en Vaderland!* As I grew older I was brought along to carry the extra copies.

"Now stand up, Tristan. Stop your slouching."

He stared down at me. With measuring eyes. Like clocks: human and mechanical, both. I could feel the sweep of his suspicions passing over me and then across the wall of the brick building behind us. I lifted my stack of papers, higher, while he reached his out to the people hurrying past us with their noses down in the wind, as if they

didn't see us, or didn't want to see us, or didn't recognize us. Until an
SS man strolled by in his long flapping coat. Then these men and
women took the papers from us and stuffed them hurriedly into their
pockets. A few would even stop to ask my father questions.

"And the Jewish banks?" demanded one stiff woman.

"That money was stolen. Everyone knows that. It was black market money. It didn't belong to them. So in justice, they had to hand
it over."

"And what's happened to all that money now? Where did it go?"

"It went to the People and the Fatherland."

"And after the war?"

"Things won't be the same after the war. The problem is almost
contained. The Jews are all living and working together, where they
can only leech from each other. They're all in Eastern Germany."

"Have you ever been to Eastern Germany?"

"No."

"It's a crime," she said accusingly. Then turned. "This keeping
your boy standing out in the cold."

"He's strong enough."

"Is he?"

"Just watch." He shoved his fist into the small of my back. I didn't
move.

Let Isolde see that, I held my chin up. Let her parade in her new
uniform, sing songs in her schoolbook German, practice with the
teacup from the new tea set, dance to the German records as if every
march were following her, but let her also know that I could stand in
an icy street in a bitter wind, and not be moved. Let her try and imagine she was still the stronger one.

When I thought of my sister's defection that way, I hardly felt it.

———

BY THE MORNING of St. Nicholas Day 1943, the cold and bitterness had become so steady they no longer inspired me. I woke up and managed to scramble out of bed for the first time before Isolde did. But found no candy stuffed inside our shoes left by the coal stove, and the grate nearly empty.

"Licorice is for babies, anyhow," she yawned and pretended not to care when she came out. She was so tall and thin her legs stuck out like a gull's under her nightgown.

"You don't know what you're talking about." I frowned.

"Black Peter must have gone to Poland."

"Don't say that!"

"You're going to cry."

"Am not."

"You're too old to cry over candy, Tristan. Just be strong, and wait."

"When do we get ours?"

"When the war's over."

"I don't want to wait anymore."

"Let's sing carols now, then." She dropped her arms by her side rigidly. "I'll start."

"You can't. You'll wake them up."

"I don't care. I want to get warm. I don't see why the soldiers don't bring us coal, anymore. We're still good people. We love our Fatherland."

"Yesterday I found ten pieces in the alley."

"Where?"

"Behind my school—I can show you." I looked up at her hopefully.

"No! I wouldn't be caught dead looking."

By that time there were also hardly any cats or dogs left in the streets. A kitten that wandered into one of the play yards was surrounded by some of the rough boys and prodded into a howling ball until one of the sharpest teachers from my school came by and scooped it up into her arms.

"Doesn't anyone have enough food at home for this poor animal? No one? Well?"

"Tristan." She saw me.

I nodded from across the street.

"Here. Hold out your arms. You take it."

"Yes, Mevrouw."

She pulled the kitten's claws from her coat and hooked them into mine. All at once I felt its sack of muscle and bone hanging from me. I held my breath. I put my hands on its striped sides, then under its wet footpads. These felt soft, like the inside of something, not its outside.

I ran home with the kitten folded close to my chest. I would show Isolde what had been conferred on me. What I had won. If she acted nicely. I would even let her touch it, if she put her hand out, softly, and said nothing cruel. I would be generous.

When I ran into the house I found my father sitting by the cold stove, my mother beside him. It was the wrong time of day for him to be there.

"What filth is that?"

"It's mine. I won it."

"Take it away."

"I can't. I have to take care of it."

"Get rid of it, I said."

"Do what your father says, Tristan."

"But I can't. I have to feed it. Mevrouw said so."

"We have to *feed* it?" my father choked. "Give our last crumb to vermin?"

"Do what your father says."

"I can't." I buried my face against the kitten's struggling nose. "It's too late."

"Tomorrow then," my mother told me. "You'll take it back tomorrow."

"Don't coddle them that way! I said he's putting the thing out, now. I won't have parasites in the house."

"That's why he's taking it back. Tomorrow."

"Where is Isolde?" I looked up quickly.

"Staying at a friend's house tonight."

"I have to go and—"

"No! How long does a man have to put up with this? With the stinking bombers out every night, and one of them always out acting like it's a party—"

"Take that animal to your room, Tristan. Clean up its messes and be quiet."

"But Mama, can I give it some—"

"No."

I slept that night with its weight circled heavily on my chest. Breathing its breath into my nose. In the morning, outside the school-yard fence, sniffling, I handed it back to Mevrouw, who blinked at me from under her sharp hat.

"You can't do it?"

I shook my head.

"You know what will happen now."

"I don't care."

That year, the canals froze. The ice was as thick as a coffin. The barges with food couldn't get through, stuck in the rivers at all angles. People ate what they could find, cats and dogs, rats and tulip bulbs, raw and dirty because there was no heat to cook them, no coal, no electricity, no wood, and no running water. But we ate no rats or cats. Before the great Hunger Winter set in, before people realized the war would not be ending that year, and that the streets had been hung too early with orange banners, we had fled to Germany.

THERE ARE POINTS so unexpectedly lowering in one's life that glancing up again the world looks as strange as a foreign and mountainous country. I stared at the walls of my flat. Since my return from the LifeCare Center, I hadn't stirred beyond them. I told myself there was nothing for it but to try to do some work.

Yet everything that might have settled me once more into my existence seemed cold, neglected, unapproachable. Even my specimens drew away from me, withering inside their shells under my attempts at concentration.

The shock of what had happened—that had settled. But now, it interposed itself between my brain and the simplest of gestures. While I brushed my teeth I thought of her face as I had last seen it. Its patina of resignation. But what did she look like, this minute? Had those eyes widened permanently with joy? At Sandor's word? Yes. And the weight had very likely melted from her cheeks. And some suppressed, conjugal pulse was again throbbing down the length of her white neck, and rushing into those long, elegant hands.

I would pick up the telephone and forget which number I had meant to dial, or why. Then find myself guessing helplessly at the sound of that voice now filling her ear, wondering if it would be, was perhaps already again, able to make her laugh and toss her head back, freely, in some way I had never even glimpsed.

I set the receiver down. What was there to say, in any case? What salutation equal to a miracle? I stayed low in my chair.

The injustice of happiness, I brooded—and let several more days pass. *How it washed over one and passed beyond and through itself up on a farther shore.* Because randomness was incapable of even the smallest concessions.

But still I believed she would have to call. She owed me that much, I felt. For my graciousness. For my restraint. For my tact. My decency, in spite of everything. She would soon—it was impossible to believe otherwise—in some quiet, reserved moment, think of me. Of course. And then on her, at last, would fall the burden of apology.

꙰

U N A B L E   T O   K E E P   S T I L L , I dusted the apartment three times. Wiping a dishcloth over every surface—my books, my collection, my dining table, my television, my journals, my kitchen counter—forcing myself at first to turn away from the harp chair, demoted to its former position at the end of the row of cabinets; then giving in, and rubbing down its arms and its curved back and bending to polish its bare, curled feet, feeling dizzy with the sudden change in altitude—a noise hissing in my head when I straightened up again.

A week had gone by. It had been a week, I knew, because there was almost nothing left to cook in the kitchen. I went on ignoring my messages and mail while copies of the *Times* piled higher on my desk.

Eventually I had no choice but to register it was no longer seven days, but twelve. Still, there was no good reason to go outside, no, not yet, not yet, not while something might still reasonably be expected. Two more days passed. Then three. Then four.

When I could no longer tolerate the silence, I unplugged the telephone to demonstrate to the walls my independence.

M Y   S T O M A C H   F I N A L L Y   D R O V E   M E from the building. Dragging myself out into the half-melted open, I realized nothing had changed. I hefted my canvas bag down the sidewalk, and my feet followed one behind the other. The sun shone in its wedge plying down the middle of the street and the air was laced with fresh garbage and the rot and rebirth of the city had gone on. I could feel a certain carelessness soaking with the general sludge into my veins. It rose into my head. I tugged down my hat, to keep it in. Nothing mattered, clearly. That was the lesson. That was the moral. I would become as dull as a club. That, the proper approach: to thicken like burl at the end of life. To abandon all pretense at plasticity. I emerged from the drugstore with a month's supply of Pepto-Bismol and aspirin and antacids, and stood for a moment under its green, unruffled awning. Until a pigeon landed on its edge, and I remembered to get out of its range.

CHAPTER

28

SHE STOOD WAITING by the front door, hovering, inexhaustible, like a hummingbird.

She spun when she saw me. Her face brightened. I thought she was hugging herself, until I saw the wine bottle pressed close to her chest.

"Elida."

"There you are!"

I adjusted my groceries and fumbled in my pocket for my keys and kept my eyes shaded.

"Martens! Where have you been?"

"Nowhere. Did you just get back from Arizona?"

"Three days ago. I've been calling."

"I've been busy. I suppose you want to come up."

"If it's all right. I was a little worried—so I took a chance and came over."

"I guess you should come up then."

Energetic, bursting, nearly bouncing from the floor of the elevator, she brought out the news of her latest specimens. *Young people,* I inured myself. All alike. Obsessed with their tiny, ingrown lives. Determined to believe, to prove, they know something about the world that has never been fully understood or appreciated until the miracle of their tiny, perfect births.

Inside she set her bottle down on the scrawl of my glass dining table. "And then also, I was surprised to find a specimen of *Tegrodera aloga* so far north. The markings on its body were so pronounced. A clear cross. Wow, what happened, it looks like a mint in here."

"What have you got?"

"Zinfandel. Cheap. I wanted to thank you so much for helping me with this trip."

"I think we can just forget about that."

"No way. I'm here to shower you with gratitude. Where's your corkscrew?"

"Drawer, next to the sink."

I turned and stared down and out the window and said nothing while she scrambled my utensils noisily. How narrow the city was, I thought. How disjointed. Cars and taxis struggling in a maze down below. Only from thirty thousand feet in the air would they appear connected, as if following one another deliberately through tracks in sand.

When in fact the surface of the planet was so vast that with only a modicum of effort we should each of us be able to avoid the other.

SHE WENT ON describing the details of her trip. Flush with enthusiasm for the red canyons, the cold nights, the stars visible over the clumps of gnarled juniper, the niches and formations in eroded rock, the stillness at noon, the sky like an endless open lid. Her strategies for collecting at dusk.

"I used a combination of lights and beating. Martens," she added, settling into my sofa while she let the wine breathe. "Do you really think I could be contributing something important, this time? There's never been such a wide study of this group of imitators. I think I've even found things nobody knew existed where they existed, much less what they were up to. By the way, do you think it's possible everything mimics everything else?"

"I don't see how."

"It doesn't make any biological sense—but I've been mulling over the idea." She stood and went blithely over to the table and passed a wineglass to me, tossing her braid like an honor cord over her shoulder before raising her own. "Now, I'm going to do what I came to do. I'm going to thank you for being so patient with me. For being my touchstone. Even when I've been a millstone around your neck. I know it. All right. Drink up, before I get too emotional."

The poor vintage burned my chest and stomach before ricocheting into my head. I blinked and reached for platitudes.

"How is your family?"

"Fine."

"How is Brooklyn?"

"Still attached."

"How is your mother?"

"Martens, what's the matter?"

"Nothing."

"You're acting oddly. Are you feeling all—? Maybe I shouldn't say anything too presumptuous."

"It would probably be better if you didn't."

"I'm afraid you'll pinch my head off."

"Impossible. I lack sufficient prehensile strength."

"There. You see that? You don't like it when people get too close."

"No. I don't like assumptions."

"Well then, why don't you just tell me what's socked you under the eyes? You've seen me at some of my worst, after all."

As usual, she wasn't going to leave until she felt she had in some way attended to me. But what was this girl? A novice. A wet-eared apprentice. On the other hand, nothing really mattered at this stage.

"I lost a friend recently, Elida."

"I'm sorry. Did they pass away?"

"No," I said acerbically. "I meant, we're not speaking."

"Why not?"

"Because something incredible has happened to her."

"That doesn't make any sense. If it was so incredible, why wouldn't she want to share it with you?"

"Because you really don't need anyone else when something of this magnitude occurs."

"I see." She pondered this, seriously. "Maybe. Or maybe not. She might be embarrassed by this thing that's happened to her. I know that feeling. It's exactly like when I won my fellowship."

"No. It's exactly *not* like that."

"Then maybe she feels guilty. I did. Like I'd done something wrong, somehow."

"And what if she did?"

"You mean do something wrong?"

"Painfully."

"But if she's your friend, why would she want to hurt you?"

There was nothing at all stinging in the way this was said. Elida's large, heart-shaped face still looked up at me, sincere, through its nimbus of confused, general sympathy. She was merely doing her best.

"No reason." I fell to pieces inside.

"So, what then?"

"I—I think it's possible I've let her be mistaken in too many things."

"Can you fix that?"

"I don't know."

"Have you tried?"

"It's not that simple." I shook my head, almost pleading with her. "You're so young, you think everything comes out of people's mouths so easily."

"You shouldn't make any assumptions. I told you about my father."

"Your father?"

"The earthquake? Mexico? Nineteen eighty-five? I told you I didn't remember anything. But I do. It just doesn't come out."

"What doesn't?"

"The shitty things I don't tell anyone I remember."

My jaw swung like a useless piece of machinery in front of her.

"Elida. I'm sorry."

"It's okay."

"No, it isn't."

"It is. Really. It's my decision if I don't want to talk about it."

"Yes—but why?"

She tilted her head. Surprising me. "Fairness. Because there's no reason to yet. Because the only person it would do any good to hear that nightmare out loud right now would be me. Not you. Not my family. Not my mother. No. I couldn't do that to her."

"I see." I nodded dimly. Then, breathing faster: "Yes."

"Anyway, that's not what I meant to go on about. I only wanted"—she bent and clasped her knees, the self-conscious graduate student again—"to find out what was the matter with you. That's it. You looked a little bit sick, Martens. I really was worried."

"I think I have been sick."

"Is there something I can do?"

"You've already done enough."

"Right." She lowered her eyes, embarrassed. "I'm a royal pain, I know."

"No, no!" I reached out and brushed her shoulder, awkwardly, resuming my old habit of reassuring her. "Not at all. Tell you what—let's not get worked up any more than we already have. All right? Let's get back to why you're here."

"To tick you off?"

"No. To celebrate. You have done important work, Elida. I *am* going to be proud. You must know that."

She frowned. Her old, cautious self. "Well, but—you don't think you're being premature, do you?"

"No."

"Or overstating the case?"

"No."

She sighed, still unconvinced. "All right. But I wish I could have done some of my collecting with you. That would have made me feel clearer about isolating certain specimens, all the way around."

"Then I regret I wasn't there."

"Anyway you would have loved the desert so early in spring, Martens. So much blooming."

As if everything could be done over again. Imagine that. As if I had never seen a flowering tree before, or broken apart the rot to find the protected colony inside. Never let my eyes travel over the ground to catch the reflection of a small, armored back pursuing its limited destiny, or turned my ears toward the concentrated disharmony of a swarm.

I pictured us together, for one moment, Elida and I—climbing, gaining a rocky, red, juniper-covered rise—and then, suddenly, the earth opening out underneath us. And her hand reaching across a canyon, and pointing, and her voice proclaiming, over every sedimentary layer, what the ground was too thick to know itself.

MY FIRST TIME in the claustrophobic box frightened me. But the priest's musk, sieving through the screen, smelled reassuringly of soap and onions. I knew the old man obscured by the mesh to be basically kind, if perpetually gray-faced and tired. Then, as the war had dragged on, I had watched his deep eyes sink like shovels more deeply into his face.

"What do I do now?" I asked him, squirming.

"You know what to do, Tristan. Say, Bless me Father, for I have sinned."

"Bless me Father for I have sinned."

"Now, you tell me how long it's been since your last confession."

"But this is my first one."

"I know, my son. I'm telling you how to do it, for the next time you have occasion to be with me. Now, tell me what sins you have committed."

"What bad things?"

"Yes. Bad things."

"Do I have to?"

"Nothing bad will happen to you, my boy. I promise. Go on, Tristan. Your sins must be very small in times such as these."

Sins, it appeared, could grow smaller or bigger. I pondered this. Like coins at the bottom of a fountain.

"And can they disappear?"

"No." A weak blast of onion, a sigh, blew through the grate between us. "There are occasions when sins are drowned in other sins. But they are, always, still sins to be reckoned with. These are the times we are in now, my son."

"We are in the war for Aryan purity."

"So, you've been listening to all that, have you? And what else have you heard? Eh? When Jesus lived, you know, his country was also occupied by an army. By the Roman army. And Jesus said, 'Give Caesar what is Caesar's.' Do you remember that, Tristan? Jesus never told the people to rise up against Rome. No. Never once. Because, you see, when an army comes, it must be ordained by God, or there wouldn't be an army come to oppress us. So it's clear that we mustn't intervene, because intervention itself would then be a direct, impious denial of God's will. Do you understand? It becomes our duty to submit. Or does it? Does it?" He drew closer to the screen between us, his hollow cheek brushing against it. "Do we follow the model of Christ's actions, or of his words?" he whispered. "Do we suffer, to let others suffer? Do we act, and bring about retribution? Do we do nothing, and pray for help? Is this the work of God? Is this the time before Time? Must we only watch, and wait?" He breathed in and coughed. I thought he must have swallowed something stronger than an onion. "Is the waiting the sin? Which is the sin?"

"Sometimes I don't wash my hands before dinner," I tried to clarify matters.

"I'm not sure"—he pulled himself back—"we can count that as something venal at this time. What else?"

"I fight with my sister."

"What about?"

"She never likes to go out hunting for things with me, anymore. She likes the girls better, in her brigade. She acts conceited, and calls me names."

"That's not your sin, Tristan."

"Can't you make her stop?"

"I can look into it. Other bad things you can think of?"

"She acts like all the new toys are hers."

"*Not* your sister's acts, Tristan. Those are between her and God. What *you* have done. Have you taken the Lord's name in vain?"

"No."

"Abused your body?"

"No." I glanced up. The top of the confessional was solid, impenetrable wood.

"Used a filthy word?"

"No."

"Disobeyed your mother or father?"

I shook my head.

"Well, then. It's a simple case. Wash your hands and stop fighting with your sister." I waited, uncertain, while he bowed his head, mumbled unintelligibly, and made the sign of the cross over me. "All right. Now, go home with your mother, and say five Hail Marys, to improve your humility before Heaven. Go on, Tristan. But be careful. Go quickly. It's getting on toward curfew, isn't it?"

"Yes, Father."

The small door shut behind me with an echo that shot up into the rafters, through the shrapnel holes opening out in the stained glass.

WANDERING HOME after school I sometimes cut across a field of rubble that before the Occupation had been a druggist's shop. The bricks and stones there lay in rounded piles and dunes. I climbed onto the rubble one afternoon—no one was watching me—to look for shell casings to show off to Isolde. Instead, my eye caught a bright piece of metal molten into a shape like a crucifix, or something like a Fokker, with short, crushed wings. I picked it up excitedly and put my arms out and flew down the side of the hill. At the bottom, I stopped. An abandoned shoe rested in front of me. I studied this. It wasn't clear if it had been a man's or a woman's. Its heel and tongue were missing, and the laces, tangled and curled off to one side, were stiffened and glistening with something sticky, like tar. I bent closely toward it. Then ran away.

The well of that shoe was filled with blood.

"LOWENSTEIN'S Fine Antiques and Reproductions."

"Is Ms. Lowenstein in?"

"She isn't. Can I take a message, please?"

"This is Dr. Tristan Martens."

"Doctor. Yes. She's only coming up in the evenings now. I can have her call you—or you can try back later?"

"I'll try later."

I counted down the hours—each one more drawn out than the

last. I held myself back, however, calculating my arrival so that I wasn't mounting the stairs until the building was almost deserted and the lights beginning to dim in the warren of businesses. Hesitating outside the shop, I peered in at my mother's table, still sitting, small and illuminated, at the end of its aisle. I felt myself cornering it, as though even now I was afraid we might elude each other. Then I straightened. Cora was coming. She spotted me only after she had drawn out her keys to close the shop.

"Tristan!"

Her eyes widened. She stood in front of me. So tall, and graceful. And yet unfamiliarly unkempt. Her silver hair tousled and shining. For a moment I thought all the resolve would drain out of me.

"Cora. Wonderful! I hoped I might catch you here tonight." I held my hand out warmly, as though we were simply acquaintances.

"I didn't expect this—I'm so glad."

She squeezed and let go of my fingers, awkward. She who was so rarely out of poise or unprepared.

"Tell me quickly," I said. "How is he?"

"It's really happened. It's a true recovery."

"That is such news."

"It's still hard, but so far things have been very steady. There's a tiny improvement, every day. He was able to hold his head up on his own this morning."

"It's almost too good to take in. You must be with him nearly constantly."

"Yes. Only recently I've started to come in late in the day, like this. Because there's so much to do. I've decided—we've decided to unload the shop."

My heart flew over a beat.

"That makes sense. You have so much more that's important to concentrate on, right now."

She nodded. She was watching me closely. "That's it."

"You'll be selling your things, then?"

"Almost everything. But let's not keep on standing here. Come in." I followed her into the shop. It was clear she was leading me toward her office. I hurriedly scanned the floor crowded with vanities.

"Let's stay out here, Cora. In front, with all your pieces. Before they go. If you don't mind?"

"Of course not."

"Are those all right to sit down in?" I was making my way toward two finely cracked chairs set close to my mother's table.

"If you're not too discriminating." She smiled. "They're reproductions."

"They look honest enough to me."

We sat down on the petit point and squandered several minutes in talking about embroideries. For a moment the air seemed clotted with woven fabrics. Then I managed to clear my throat.

"Cora. I want you to know I'm so very happy for you."

"Are you?" she asked frankly.

My plan had been to rush down the straight road as far as I could. This brought me up short.

"I didn't mean it that way," she added quickly.

"No. It's all right."

"I'm not sure I'm being fair to you, Tristan. I'm not sure I'm being fair to Sandor. This is all so complicated. I wonder if I'm being incredibly—dense."

"You aren't wondering that. You can't. You know you've done absolutely nothing wrongheaded."

"Why haven't you called?"

"Because I couldn't."

"You felt I'd been using you."

"Never. Never. I couldn't even imagine that. That's absurd."

"Don't try to dismiss any of this, please. Be my friend."

"But I don't know if I should be, anymore."

"That's exactly what I mean by dense—I still want you to be. I'm fixed on it. So what does that tell you?"

"That you never give up."

"No. It tells you that I'm willing to be incoherent. Unreasonable. That I want everything to be possible at the same time."

Her words gave me the encouragement I needed. "That doesn't matter. It's only human. You have to see that the wrong is all someplace else. That's what I wanted to talk to you about. It has been, for a long time."

"I don't know what you mean."

"Please, Cora, I didn't mean to hurt you by not calling."

"I was afraid you did."

"I know I've hurt you. But not in the way you think. Because I've lied to you more than you might have thought possible."

"We've already put those things behind us."

"No, we haven't. My parents were Nazis, yes. My sister was what you know. But there's more, Cora. That table, right there, was in our house. And the writing underneath it is mine. It's half mine. You've got to hear this. It's the reason we're talking together right now."

She remained perfectly still. Like my oldest image of her: the dream of a frozen ship. And yet, while I watched, without a trace of emotion or motion she carefully recomposed herself in her chair. And there she held. The Cora I had expected, and counted on, and hoped would stay long enough to let me finish.

"I don't understand you, Tristan. I want to understand. But I have to know what on earth it is you imagine you're talking about."

"I know. That's why I think it's best we're sitting down."

CHAPTER

3 0

"THAT WAS MY MOTHER'S WORKTABLE. In our house in Rotterdam. My sister and I used to hide and play games under it. We wrote the words together. *Als de Joden weg zijn is het onze beurt.* We learned slogans like that, and more, from our father. I couldn't tell you. I was too ashamed. And so foolish. I thought if we got to know each other, if you thought I was honorable, and worthy, you'd let me buy it from you and take it away from you without my ever having to let you know what it was. I was using you to get to it. At first."

I hurried. "You can't imagine how crazed it made me to see it again. It just wasn't possible. Near the end of the war, we started packing for Germany—my mother was German—but we only took what we could carry, and as soon as we got away from the house the neighbors came in and tore apart everything. I saw them throwing all the furniture out, everything, before we made it twenty paces toward the train station. I thought that was the end of it. I remember jumping out and hiding on the tracks under the train whenever the bombs started falling, and every time we got back into the car finding more of our belongings stolen. At the border we had so little left the Germans didn't even want to let us through. My mother had to bribe a guard with a butter knife."

I watched my mother, at the last station the bombed line could carry us to, slapping her cold hands in her armpits and bargaining with a driver who owned a cart, pointing and deciding something with him and without consulting my father. She gave the man another piece of silverware. Then we were loaded onto his wagon behind his decrepit horse. And were driven through the once-imagined land of honeybees. Past a few filmy-eyed cows. Grapevines curled dismally out on wires, like charred snakes. A woman stood by the side of the road and clapped her hand to her mouth as we went by.

"We're more bad news," my mother said.

Her sister looked unimpressed to see us. She said we could have the barren farm, for all she cared. "My boys are dead. Almost everything else, too." She shrugged carelessly. "I don't know what any of us are waiting for, now."

My father stayed inside, hunched by the radio in the kitchen. My mother's face grew redder from working in the patchy garden trying to pull up enough roots to thicken a dinner to feed all of us. Isolde complained that everything in the country was dirty and poor and ugly and stinking and disgusting—and on her fifteenth birthday, when she got no presents or poems from any of us, even I felt sorry for her, and tried to get her to sing. But she cursed me and ran off and disappeared.

We weren't watched very carefully. There was no work to ask us to do. We weren't sent to school. I spent my time chasing the goats too thin to milk or eat, or rolling on the floor with my aunt's black hound, who slept in the kitchen and bared his teeth at the sound of planes or artillery. Isolde would disappear down the long town road and not come back until her mood had changed and she was happy and smiled and said she'd been out gossiping with the Reuber girls.

"Hussy," shrugged my aunt.

By the time the Allied planes flew so thick and slow over the house pieces of plaster slid from the walls like melting snow, we knew the war was over. My father switched off the radio.

"That's it then."

"They'll be coming to find us," predicted my mother.

"Don't be ridiculous. Everything's total chaos. You're German, and we have German papers. No one will know. The trick is to act normally. Like we belong here. We have to behave that way. Tristan, let me hear your German."

"May I go outside and play with the dog?"

"Isolde."

"I'm going to go over to the Reubers' house."

"Don't be so smug about it, girl. Don't try to act like you're so much better than everyone else."

The two stringy goats died, that summer. I found one lying stiffly in the field, its lips reared back from its teeth, as though it could smell itself going putrid. My aunt said they'd been poisoned by Americans. But I was worried I had done it. That I had chased and pulled on their stubbed horns too often. That I didn't know how to be a good country boy. I was supposed to start in a German school, the next year, and then everyone would discover I wasn't a good country boy, but a goat murderer.

I stayed near the house after that, pitching rocks over the low roof, throwing my weight against the fence posts. All at once I missed my bed-closet in Rotterdam, my collection of shrapnel, the ugly, snouted coal stove, the sound of Isolde's heavy breathing in the next room. Now I stood helpless at the edge of a strange yard, tugging at a rotten log. I wanted to pull it out and see it fall over like a dead tree stump and uproot the ant bed at its base, but it wouldn't topple. Then I caught sight of Isolde starting up across the field, and raced to follow her.

"Where are you going?"

"Nowhere." Her arms were sunburned.

"To the Reubers'?"

"Maybe."

"Can I come?"

"No."

"Why not?"

"You wouldn't like it. It's something for grown-ups."

"I'll do what I want to. I can now."

"So what? Anybody can."

"You're wearing lipstick." I recoiled.

"What do you know about it?"

"You got it from Hibi Reuber."

"No, I didn't. I got it from one of those boys staying with them. One of the soldiers who ran away. Now go away."

"No." I didn't want to leave her side.

"I said to."

"You can't make me."

"Yes, I can." She wrenched my arm back in a twist-grip and pulled me to a standstill and bent down so that her face was next to mine.

I hated Isolde then. She had gotten so tall, so tall, pulled up like a ladder into a loft I couldn't reach. I struggled.

"If you were me," she whispered suddenly, "you'd be doing the same thing."

"I hate you. I don't love you."

"Don't make me hurt you any harder than this, Tristan. You have to stop following me. Just go back."

"No. I'll tell."

"Tell what? You don't know anything about it. You wait. Until it happens to you. Then you'll see. It's like getting born again." She tossed my elbow away, leaving me dizzy. "Helmut says so, too. The war is dead. And as far as I'm concerned everything about it can just rot and stink and go to hell." I saw something in her face that was new and pink.

"You sound stupid," I flailed jealously.

"I don't care what anyone says." I watched her skirt balloon above her high socks as she ran. Then, I counted to fifty in German. Then walked slowly back, between the fence posts, into the yard, and across the path to the kitchen where my father sat.

"Isolde is down on the town road again with a soldier."

"What, you say?"

"Isolde is down on the town road again with a soldier."

"Doing what?"

"Fucking," I pronounced carefully.

"Take me there!"

Isolde would be sorry now. She would be locked up in the kitchen. She would be tied down. She would have to sit in a chair, and sew patches. I hurried over the field toward the town road. I could feel every blade of grass licking against the holes in my shoe leather. The wind whipping me like a flag. I went faster. My father, stooped from his weeks in his chair, could hardly keep up. When we spotted them they were already walking along one of the thickening vineyards, arms linked. The soldier was thin and hobbled on a bad leg and his country disguise hung on him like a scarecrow's. The wind kept pushing them farther ahead of us. I could see their knees buckling with the pressure from behind.

My father shoved me up against a tree. "Stay here." He waited to let them get farther ahead, then followed them down the road.

I waited. I couldn't hear anything with the wind blowing past me. But I could see my father when he stopped behind them and stuck his neck out and shouted something. I watched them wheel at this. The soldier wavered and almost jumped onto his bad leg. Isolde stepped back. My father shouted something again. She took another step back, away from him. He spat something, and pointed at her, and then at the soldier. Now Isolde shouted back. She leaned into the wind, and her mouth was round and hard and her face was red as she held on to the soldier's hand behind her and pulled against him, like a rope about to snap. My father stepped in toward her. And slapped her. I couldn't hear the sound. None of them moved. Then he turned and pointed up at me.

I stood with my feet planted, steadily. My ears burned with excitement. The soldier shouted and called Isolde something now and wrenched his hand from hers and threw it up into the air as if he'd had enough, as if he could take no more, and then he shouted again at her and my father both and turned and cut grotesque and hobbling and thrashing through a row of vines, and disappeared. Isolde started after him but my father grabbed her and spun her around at the shoulders and shoved her back up the road. She rushed ahead of him, climbing. I could see her trying to hold her chest and head up, her face coming closer now, her cheeks wet, her blond hair matted in her eyes. I stood my ground, under my tree. My heart thumped like a drum.

"Are you satisfied now," she hissed into my ear as she passed. "You killed it."

I didn't understand what she meant. But it didn't worry me, then. She had to stay on the farm for weeks after that, so I was pleased. She had to sit still in a chair, and darn socks. Under the table between us, words passed without being spoken. Mine was at last the upper hand.

I didn't understand what I had done or what had happened, even when two men came to the kitchen door and Isolde, without looking at my father, stood up and walked over to them and calmly told them our family name and history. "We are Dutch Nazis," she said. I didn't understand, not fully, even when we were put on the train for Westerbork and taken off and hosed down and coated with DDT. Not even when we were separated and carted away in the ambulance and then left standing, the three of us, in the prisoners' hotel in our rooms on the fifth floor, when my mother dropped our single bag and stared at the damp running down the peeling walls, and at the furniture missing some of its legs.

"This is what you get from living with men without balls," she said.

During that first night I couldn't find a soft place on the bad mattress. I could hear Isolde's breathing, light and even above my mother's, through the door, in the next room. She must have been planning, even then, as though it were some long-ago St. Nicholas Eve, to get up before any of the rest of us could. But I didn't know or understand this. I fell asleep, and didn't hear her in the morning when she rose and put on her shoes, didn't hear her close the door and walk down the hallway and then, at the end of it, open a window and stand on the sill, hovering on one foot for an instant before she shouted *All this makes me sick!* and jumped and cracked her head like a doll's against the curb.

My mother swore to everyone she had fallen. The priest came to our rooms to console us, but my mother grabbed at his collar before he could pray and dropped to her knees, rocking, explaining, keening, insisting that he had to allow Isolde to be buried in a Catholic cemetery. Even though everyone in that hotel knew my sister had shouted *Ik word er doodziek van!* so the world would know exactly what she had thought of the wet, peeling walls.

At the cemetery, facing the hole in the ground and the black plug of her coffin, I stood by my mother's side, trembling.

"It's so terrible, Tristan. Your sister had to go to hell. Why did she have to do it? It's all her fault."

I ran away then from that falsely consecrated grave. Because finally I understood. My mother was wrong. Though I said nothing about it—then or afterwards. Because there was nothing left to say. And no God worth saying it to. Not then. Not later, not after the pictures of the piled bodies, the pictures my parents shook their heads over in denial. No crime that had not already been committed. What dispensation would ever allow me to name my guilt and shame and despair over my sister? What right did I have to speak, when I had killed some faint hope for her, and the bodies had already been piled so high, in Birkenau, in Dachau, in Buchenwald? When the earth was full of silent creatures already gnawing and doing their work, and there could be no hope of forgiveness, every eye already turned, understandably, and lowered. Every ear already placed in anguish to the ground.

I STOPPED, unclear if I had really spoken. The chair across from me creaked slightly, a tuning of strong wood. This told me I had done it.

"Oh, Tristan." Cora held her long hands open on her lap to show me. "It wasn't your fault. You were just a child."

"I knew what I was doing."

"You didn't."

"The heart knows its own history."

"It does," she sighed. "That's why it takes someone else to be the judge of it."

We sat next to each other. No closer than we had been an hour before. And yet so close, I understood, it could only be because something complex had grown and twined a screen between us, making it possible for us to be together.

"What," I wondered, "do we do now?"

"I think we go out, and get something to eat."

"Cora."

"I know. I know. Tell me what you need, first."

"You'll keep it?"

"I will."

"And the details, they'll be told? If anyone asks."

"They will be."

"And you'll tell Sandor?"

"Yes. Though I hope you'll be telling him yourself one day, if there's any sense to the world." She paused. "Just let me lock a few things up in my desk. And then we'll go."

As we rose she surprised me with a brief embrace. I felt the fine wings of her hair against my cheek. But the moment was over before I had time to absorb all its fineness.

She left me then and slipped back down the aisle and with a mechanical gesture pulled the door of her office closed behind her. From where I stood, alone beside my chair, I saw the light switch on, and, from underneath the door, spread in a narrow moat across the floor between us.

I had already decided, hours before, that the truth would have to be left behind, on this night. But now my heart seized and faltered, trying to defeat me. I wanted to give up, and follow her. I wanted so much more from her than company. I struggled with my heart. And the moment passed.

A C K N O W L E D G M E N T S

Mijn hartelijke dank to Greg Michalson, especially; to Margie Kalhorn, mother strong and loving; to Fred Ramey, Paul Chung, Dr. Duco van Oostrum, Dr. Nancy Greig, Debbie Lee Wesselmann, Laurel Doud, Cynthia Mott, Shaun Burnett, Roxanne Ray, and Weezie Mackey; to the work of Arthur Evans, Charles Bellamy, Bob Moore, Floyd Werner, Sigmund Eisner, Richard E. White, and Edward O. Wilson, among many others; to the University of St. Thomas for time during the early going; but most of all to Dennis, beginning and end, always.